I woke up one night, and I couldn't go back
to sleep. A question out of thin air had
interrupted my peace. What was
my purpose? What had I done with what
God had blessed me with? What had I done
to say thank you for all the mercy that
was bestowed upon me? This question
invaded my privacy, my safe place. I
started feeling nervous; I was panicking. I
prided myself on being intelligent. I
prided myself on having composure. As
the questions piled up, if it was a test, I
would fail. I studied myself, and I had to
pass this test. My future sanity depended
on it. What did I have to give, a twenty-
seven-year-old convicted felon with more
time to do than I had lived? I had a duty; I
had to find the reason I existed, the reason I
had been through all I had been through.
Why I had to see these lows that life had to
offer. What was the ending to this story
because I knew I wasn't worthless? I've
always felt the presence of my worth. Or
maybe I was worthless. I had to find the

answers to these questions. Laying on a top bunk of a level four max facility prison, I did an inventory of my valued possessions. At the very top was my support system, the people I knew who prayed for me. I had my love and my mind and the vastness of it. I had a unique thought process and a very active imagination. I had my pain; it was a prize to me because of all I had learned from it. I had my story, what I learned from all my mistakes. I thought hard on how I could bottle this up and package it for the world. I had found my purpose, but being incarcerated, how do I make it come to life? That's when I knew I had to use my most prized possession, my family. I had the vision; I had the resources. In prison, you never run out of pen and paper. I even knew I was dedicating my purpose to. I could remember when I needed the most help. I couldn't save myself per say, but I could reach and try to save someone like me. A young lost soul with too many questions and not enough answers and no warnings that resonated to me. I had the want to reach and was blessed with a twin sister, so when my two arms were shackled and chained, my two other arms could carry the load. That's where my sister, my better half comes in. I would need her arms, but when you have positivity in your heart, arms will come out of nowhere to carry your vision.

Interactive reading

You will notice highlighted red words in this book. When you see them ask Alexa or your home service device such as Siri Alexa, etc., and explore the knowledge on the spot and enjoy a little music to help you along the journey.

Acknowledge

I want to personally thank God 1st and foremost for never leaving my side even through the darkest parts of my journey! I want to thank Vernon Bateman for showing me who I can be! I want to give thanks to Calvin Lyons, Leroy Jones, Dion Beals, Devin Brookins and D'cartia Hoskins for investing in my growth! I wanna thank all my nieces and nephews for loving and encouraging me. I wanna also thank my inspiration the lights of my light Kai, RJ, Asher, and Lillie they are what makes me get out of the bed and work on me being a better me. Last but not least I wanna thank my Queen without her this would be impossible she made this dream come to life.

CHAPTER 1

Destiny's head popped up from under the covers. Her little hand reached to her dresser as her mother, Jasmine giggled." Girl, you act like you got some business." Destiny put her lock code into her phone. "Girl, what do you need a lock on your phone for?" Destiny rolls her hazel green eyes. "Cuz Future nosey and I have a right to privacy." You have a right to get your butt up and brush your teeth. Now get ready for school and get breakfast." Future jumped out of the top bunk "I heard bacon; that's all the motivation I need!" Jasmine couldn't believe how big they had gotten when the twins were born; they looked so much alike that she really had to look at them to know who was who? Future had big, beautiful eyes and lashes, topped with a full head of curly hair. They both had their granny eyes; Destiny's eyes changed with the season. Their smooth caramel skin came from Jasmine's side of the family. Destiny was growing to be her spitting image, while Future looked like his father when he was young, just a long lankier version. The twin's father, Ro, said that Future took after his brother. Their kids looked so much like each other, and like them, Jasmine and Ro started to think they looked alike. "It's like you grow an inch a week. And do something with your hair. You look like a chi-chia pet." "What's a chi-chia pet?" Future asked. Huh, Jasmine paused. "I'm getting old. Come on y'all; I can't be late for work. And tonight, daddy is coming to get you, so don't be playing around after school." Jasmine wasn't where she wanted to be in life, but she enjoyed her little world with her kids. They lived in a small, comfortable apartment, but she was planning on getting a house this year. She knew that the twins were getting big and needed their own bedrooms, but she was stuck in her ways. She wanted a complete family before she purchased a house. She was only missing the husband; then everything would be perfect. "Come on, you two," Jasmine yelled again. "That's Destiny, ma; she thinks the bathroom is her dressing room." " Come on, if I'm late I'mma sell tickets for the royal rumble we are going to have." "Mom, stop being dramatic," Destiny sighed as they headed for her car; Jasmine knew that she needed a new one. Her maroon minivan screamed, "soccer, mom!" Her first kids had been twins; she may have overreacted, but that seemed so long ago. They all piled into the van, school-bound.

CHAPTER 2

"Love you, mom." "Love you, Destiny. And don't be on your phone in class." "Bye, mama Sista. Mwah as Future kissed his mother. Love you, baby. Don't be late; your daddy is coming to get you two." Ok, both replied as Future ran to the school doors, and Destiny walked off with her friends. Destiny's friends were considered pretty girls. Chanelle looked like a miniature Rihanna and was spoiled to the core. She loved being mixed with Brazilians and was not scared to let everyone know. Paris was biracial. Her daddy was an ex-NBA player, and her mom was a chef. The trio was a walking teen tabloid. "Hey girl," Chanelle said as Destiny walked up. Hey, Chanelle, your hair is so cute, "Destiny replied." "I saw your post. Is your dad coming this weekend? "You're gonna miss Jessie's pool party," Paris chimed in. "Not for the world! I got my dad in the palms of my hand, he'll bring me, and my swimsuit will be the talk of the year." Chanelle, Destiny, and Paris started walking towards their lockers to get their books for their first class. Hey Destiny? Jessie and his group of friends walked up. Jessie was a head taller than Destiny and all her friends.

He was almost taller than everybody at the school but Future. He had the clearest skin with the whitest teeth Destiny had ever seen. She thought he had the perfect skin color, not too light but not too dark. Not to mention, he dressed like he had a personal stylist.

Will you sit by me at lunch? You can bring your cheerleaders. Jessie's friends laughed. Destiny blushed. Chanelle snapped her neck. "Don't be cute, Jessie." The bell rang, signaling the start of class. I gotta go; I hope to see you at lunch. Jessie and his friends walked away. Destiny looked at Chanelle. "What do you mean, don't be cute? That's impossible for him." Destiny, Paris, and Chanelle chuckled as they headed to the first period. "Quiet class, quiet. Today we're learning about the constitution. Get your books out and turn to page 30. While you all turn to the page, I need you to pass up last night's homework. Mrs. Tibbs waited as they did as they were told. Future went in his backpack and pulled his homework out. He knew he was going to get an (A) because history was his favorite subject. Future leaned over and whispered, "Did you do your homework, Worm?" Nope was up binge-watching YouTube fights." Worm was a scrawny little boy of bones with a unibrow. The name worm was given to him in kindergarten when kids called his unibrow a worm on his face. He said that he kept it to be like Anthony Davis, his favorite basketball player. "Dang, Worm, you gonna fail all yo classes." Who needs class? I'mma be a UFO fighter. Bro, you take classes too serious; you don't need to know history; bro, you are going to the league." " I like history, and I'm not going anywhere if I don't make my grades. "Bro, Worm whispered with pity, you starting to sound lame. You can google everything she got to teach. I don't have to remember anything. Mrs. Tibbs thumbed through the stack of papers. I see you did your homework, Future. Yes, ma'am, Future replied. "Reuben, I don't see yours. "Ugh... I lost it," Worm lied. "That's the third time this week; you must have amnesia. "I'll have today's homework, Mrs. Tibbs." I know, she replied I'm calling your mom tonight. "Ha-ha, Future quietly laughed. You're doing homework tonight, Reuben! "Shut up, and it's Worm to you." Mrs. Tibbs started writing on the board. Can anybody tell me what year the constitution was written? Hmm? Taylor? It was written in 1787. Good. Today we're going to explore the importance the constitution has on your lives.

CHAPTER 3

History report. She wants us to write a history book; it is more like it," worm complained. Shut up, worm. You gonna lose it anyway. "What up, Future? What's brackin, Worm?" "What up, Varis? Varis was trouble wrapped in skin. He had muscles, unlike a football player, slimmer like Bruce Lee. He even had a tattoo already. His knuckles were scarred, but his face was smooth as a baby's. You knew he was a problem at one glance. His skin was like a penny, and his dreads never looked done. He was not to be messed with and had been proving that since third grade. Nothing, Varis replied. Dang, Future last game was 20 points. You were balling! Thanks, bro. Future said nervously. You know what they say, if you can hoop, you can fight. Varis throws a play jab. Worm was already finna get down with the set. You know the rules of the streets: rap, ball, or gang bang. We always got room for a scorer." Varis and his gang started laughing. "Worm, you gonna be ready this weekend? Ain't no turning back. "I ain't a choker, I'mma be their fa-sho" "Bring Future so he can see what it takes to be a gang. I'mma catch you slime later." Varis and his gang walked away. Future punched Worm in the arm. Ouch! What was that for? Future's face was serious. Gang? Dude, Varis don't play about that. His great-great granddaddy was slime. You are not built for that life. Speak for yourself. I'm not finna be out here alone. You're lucky you can go to your Pop's. Mine's dead, who gone protect me and make sure I got someone to call on? No one. So, I might as well start early, so I ain't gotta prove myself later. That's the dumbest thing I heard you say, and I heard you say a lot of dumb stuff. "Well, think about it like this, I might be dumb, but I ain't gone be weak or weird." The bell rang. "Well, I'll see you at lunch, I got math. Pray for me.

CHAPTER 4

"Can I get a slice of pizza, Apple Juice, and a Buffalo sauce? "Destiny, I swear you eat the nastiest stuff." Shut up, Chanelle, Destiny retorted; pizza and hot sauce is good! "More like ghetto." Come on, Paris is holding our table. "I'm not sitting with ya'll; I been invited to a dinner date." Pizza and tater tots more like a snack date; Chanelle laughed, and Destiny rolled her green eyes. Jealous, Destiny snapped. Jealous? For what? I'm coming with you. They both start laughing. Jessie and his friends were all in the back of the cafeteria, where all the popular kids hung out, and everyone else stayed clear. Destiny, Chanelle, and Paris, who had just joined them, walked up to Jessie's table. "Make room heathens," they demanded. Jessie smirked. "Destiny, come sit next to me, he called." Let me get some of yo buffalo sauce." Ugh, you too. Chanelle muttered. A match made in project heaven. Jessie threw a tater tot at Chanelle. "Boy, stop! "So Destiny, Jessie says, facing her, you know my pool party gone be turnt. It's gone be a fashion show." You turning thirteen, what are you getting, a car? You know your parents spoil you. Destiny said playfully; you got jokes. You know my pops take good care of me. But material things are nothing. All I want for my birthday is more time with you. Jessie said, turning his charm on. Stop it. Destiny's caramel blushes. "You got plenty girls." Yea, but I really kinda sort of want you. He whispered. Eat your lunch." You might be hungry or thirsty." Girl, you are really funny. But for real. What's your number? "How you like me so much but don't have my number. Destiny teased. Destiny pulled her phone out. What you gone save my number as? Jessie asked. Jessie, your name. "Let me see; Jessie quickly took her phone. Boy, don't snatch from me. That's not nice. Destiny covered her face to hide from blushing. He had saved her name under the heart emoji. " Look, Destiny, your brother finna fight! A crowd had formed around Future and Worm. The school loved nothing more than a good fight. Kids had their phones out, waiting for the action to start. Destiny ran through the crowd." Cuz, you think because you can hoop, you God? Quise asked." You bumped into me; Future shot back." Ain't my fault you are clumsy. "You can play ball, but we gone see if you can fight!" "Hey, bro, we ain't gotta fight. He's sorry, Worm said. Worm, I'm not sorry, he bumped into us! "Just calm down, "Worm counseled," we can talk this out. Meanwhile, out of nowhere, Varis and his gang slid up, between future and Quise." I have been waiting for you to mess up, Quise. Varis said. "Cuz, this ain't got nothing to do with you," Quise replied. "First off, watch yo mouth. I'm big slime to you, and this is my school. You know you crabs don't stand on anything." More of Quise guys came up. "Enough talking. Let's see who stands on what." Varis punched Quise square on the jaw, starting a full-blown brawl. Destiny snatched Future by the backpack. "What's wrong with you? She yelled over the noise. Come on! Future and Destiny managed to get to the hallway before the teachers got involved.

"Thanks, sis, but Quise was tripping." You gotta be smarter. That turned into a gang fight. That ain't you, is it? "That's Worm. He got something going on with them." Future told his sister. "You can't get involved in that," Destiny replied. "Go to class; I'mma see you after school.

CHAPTER 5

The final bell rang. "Alright, class, make sure you remember your homework, the teacher called out. The bell meant the weekend, and the kids started a stampede in a mad dash to get home and get their weekend started. "Paris, let me copy your notes. "Ok, girl, hurry up! Look at this, Destiny. This is so cute. I wish my mom would let me wear this to Jessie's party." Destiny took the phone and liked the bikini that the model had on. The bikini was small and revealing. She knew her mother would never approve of her wearing it, but she had to find a way. "Paris, I must have one of these!" Yeah, maybe senior year of high school. What site is that? "Fashion passion." Paris replied. Ok, I'mma put in my favorites. Tell Future to stay out of trouble while you are at it. I can't marry him if he doesn't graduate from school. Destiny starts laughing. "Ok, she heads for the exit to see where her mom parked." Future. Future ay, wait up! "What you want, Worm? "Everyone is saying that the police came and picked up Quise and Varis." They always get picked up. They'll be back to school in two weeks. Future replied. See, Varis had our backs. "I don't need them to have my back; I wasn't wrong." Either way, Worm continued, "they good people to have on your side." I don't know him or need him to have my back. You don't, either. I could've been in that and gotten suspended or, worse, expelled. Future replied. Well, neither happened, Worm retorted, so calm down. What are you gonna do when Quise comes back to school, or his gang wanna finish what happened today? I don't know; I'll cross that bridge when it comes. Well, I'll catch you Monday. Just text me. They parted ways; future started towards the door to find his mom's car.

CHAPTER 6

"Hey, mom." "Hey, baby. How was your day?" Let me guess... gossip, homework, and group selfies. Destiny rolled her eyes. "How was my big man's day?" Future and Destiny met eyes. "It was cool." That's good. Ya'll make me feel like I got the best kids in the world. I grabbed ya'll bags. Ya'll daddy needs me to drop ya'll off. Destiny, I already let yo daddy know he gotta take you swimsuit shopping. And Future, he knows you got practice tomorrow afternoon. I put some of my chocolate chip cookies in both ya'll bags." Mom, those cookies gonna be gone before you pull off the block. Future a garbage disposal. "One cookie is all you gone eat the whole weekend., skeleton diet-looking self." You guys, behave. What homework you got, Future? "Nothing too difficult he replied, I got a history report." Ok. Well, call me if you need help. What about you, Destiny?" I got to study for a test, and I took notes. Hey mom? "Yes, Destiny?" Was dad your first crush? "Omg, Future sighed. I don't wanna think about you and pops kissy, Facey." Shut up, boy. And no, but he was the first person I'd been in love with." How did you know you loved him? "He gave me these butterflies that made me wanna go against all the rules." "If you felt like that, then why didn't you stay with dad?" That's life and love. But he did give me you two guys. The joys of my life. I was in love at first sight. "Ma, I have seen Future's baby pictures. With that sized head, you shoulda been upset with him! Jasmine giggled." Stop talking about my baby. I love his head. Destiny was busy thinking about how she was gonna make herself Jessie's first love.

CHAPTER 7

"Is that daddy's princess? "Jasmine had to admit that Ro was a very handsome man. He was a little taller than her, about 5'6; he had a tattoo on his neck, was well built, and had a great grade of hair. He was mixed with Cuban and had a good mix of street and class. He was perfect... Until he opened his mouth." Can I get some kisses, or are you too fleek now? "Dad! Fleek is not your word, Destiny protested." What up, son? Is it me, or did you grow some more? Aw, I'm tripping. It's just that chi-chia pet. What the heck is a che-chia pet? Mom said the same thing, "Future asked, curiously annoyed. "Dang, I just felt old. Ya'll go in the house and get settled. I need a second to talk to ya'll mom. As soon as the kids made it in the house. Jasmine got straight to the point. Ro, you gotta watch Destiny when she is picking her swimsuit. She got a Lil boy she likes. "You let her have that phone; she probably already talking to boys. I'm not arguing the past; I'm talking about now. And jasmine continued. I don't want Future around here with these little thugs around your house. " All these Lil dudes ain't bad. He needs some male friends. I don't want him weird. "My baby, ok. He's on the basketball team, Jasmine countered." Yeah, but he got one friend named Worm. I don't want him to be Socially awkward. "Just be watching," "I always watch my kids. Why can't we be civil? It would be civil if you trusted me. Ro stated. "Please don't talk about trust, Ro. "Bye, Jasmine. I'll see you Sunday night. Ro turned and walked into his little modest three-bedroom house. The kids had their own room, not like their mom's house. It was small, but it was his, and he kept his grass green and cut like his father before him.

\

CHAPTER 8

Boom. "You make me happy...the music floats through the walls. Boom. Boom. Future hops up." Dads at it again...music and pancakes." Destiny pulls the covers over her head. "Huh, this ancient music gets on my nerves." Ro yells as he passes the doors. "Come on, get up! How you start yo day is important. Good food and good vibes." Ro started to dance in front of their doors. "When ya'll was kids you loved dancing with me, and pancakes. Especially you, Destiny "Ro had his World's greatest dad apron on and he truly felt like it when he had his kids. He didn't think his kid knew the joy they gave him." Come on, Destiny! Future was laughing "dad, this is grandma music what you got going on. "Where you think I got my style from? And where you think you got your swag from? "Not from granny, I know that! Destiny finally got up " both, ya'll out of my way. As she tried to pass Ro got a hold of her. "Dance with yo old man. Come on, sing along! You make me happy. This you can tell." Ro dips Destiny she started giggling "let go, dad! "You, my princess, this how we gone dance at your wedding when you forty." You crazy, pops. I'm getting married long before forty! "Over my dead body Ro said future laughed " Well, pops, we gone have your funeral and my wedding the same day. Save some money. Destiny said laughing "That's spose to be funny? Ya'll get ready, grab some breakfast. We got some bonding to do

CHAPTER 9

"Now this that hit! Future turned the car radio up." Die! You gone die! What's this? "Ro looked at his son, disappointed. See, you old. You wouldn't understand." Trippie be going in. One: I'm not old, and two: I don't wanna understand this. So, Destiny, you wanna go to the mall or stop somewhere else? Mumbling under his breath. "I don't know why your mom ain't take you for swimsuit shopping. She knows I hate stuff like this." We can go to the mall, but we gotta be there by two. I'm trynna catch Chanelle up there. She replied. "Ok, princess." They pulled up to the school gymnasium. "I'mma be back out here at 5:00. Tell your coach I said, Hey. Work hard and push yourself, son. You're your only obstacle. Love you, boy." Love you too, pops. Bye, sis. Bye, daddy, long legs." Destiny says as Future shuts the car door." Ok, one-on-one time with my princess. Did you know I met yo mom in 8th grade? "You look just like her the first time I saw her, Ro remembered fondly." Did you know you loved her when you first saw her? Destiny was beyond curious. "Heck, he laughed; I couldn't stand her stuck-up self. But she was so different. I can't even explain it. Ro's cell phone began to ring. Hold on baby. Hello? I'm driving; let me call you when I get to where I'm going. It was never that lit. Man, you gotta tell me everything. Light bro. Destiny was checking her messages. There was a text from Jessie, good morning, with a kissy face. Hey, she texted back. "Wyd," he texted. Shopping for your gift. Better be special, Jessie texted back.

CHAPTER10

"What do you want on your ice cream, princess?" "Excuse me, frozen yogurt, Ro mocked in good nature. It's better for you than that fat-filled triple scoop you got, Destiny retorted. Just put sprinkles on hers and put chocolate chips and Carmel on mine. "OMG, dad, you're disgusting." That's my everything plus the kitchen sink mixture. When you were younger, would be wired up for two days! Ro laughed. Well, now I know what all those sugars and calories do to your body, and I want no part. And you should watch out, too, as Destiny patted his belly. "How in the world do you kids know all this? And I look good, thank you very much! How? Do you like your swimsuit? Destiny was upset. The whole time her daddy had been focused on watching her pick out and try on her swimsuit and everything. She had a worse swimsuit than if she had gone with her mother." Yea, dad, thank you so much. Destiny's phone vibrated. A text from Chanelle." Where are you? I'm here. The food court. Destiny replied. "I'm on my way; I'm with my older sister." "Come on, dad; I'm trynna meet Chanelle and her sister." Ok, princess. Chanelle was excited. "Hey girl! Hey, Destiny, Chanelle greeted more calmly. Kiesha was a beauty and was around Ro's age. I've heard so much about you. And this must be your father. Yeah, my name is Ro, he said with a smile and a nod. Kiesha, it's nice to meet you, Ro. "Trust me; the pleasures are all mine. Ro flashed his famous million-dollar smile. Kiesha started blushing as she turned toward her sister. "Okay, Chanelle, I'mma meet you back here at 3:30. Don't be lolly-gagging." Ok, Chanelle replied, with exasperation in her voice. Ro, do you know a store who got wireless headphones? I don't know, but I'll be glad to assist you in your endeavor. Destiny, you, and Chanelle, ok? "Yea, dad with a green-eyed eyeroll. "Well, I'mma help Kiesha and meet you back here." "Ok, dad," as they parted ways from the food court.

CHAPTER 11

"He was not on top of it like that." Yes, girl! He was going for none of my tricks, Destiny lamented. "I think my mom warned him." "But a one piece? Ugh, I got a two-piece at least, and I got these sunglasses and my Ri-Ri towel. Chanelle lowkey bragged." I'm glad you gone be fine, but what about me? "I don't know. Play sick?" "Girl, shut up. Destiny and Chanelle wandered into a make-up store." "I swear I don't know how I'mma get over this weekend." Which lip gloss should I get? Chanelle already had a truckload of bags hanging from her arms. You know I love cherry, but you usually get kiwi... forget it, I'mma get both." Chanelle took the two lip glosses and casually slipped them into her bag. Destiny was blown away. "Chanelle, what in the world!" Shhh, calm down, scary, Chanelle half whispered, half hissed. I do this all the time. We are young, pretty girls. They don't think anything of us. "What about if you do get caught? I can't believe you were this... Destiny stammered." "What destiny? This bad, a thief, whatever you call it? I get what I want, and I can't lie; it's fun." Come on, let's go look at some dresses or something. Destiny was quiet as she and Chanelle went store to store. A voice called out, "hey, Chanelle. I see you at it again, spoiled rotten." "Hey, miss Toliver." Who's that, Chanelle? Destiny asked. "My next-door neighbor, Chanelle replied before addressing miss Toliver again." You know I'mma good girl, so my parents reward me. Chanelle, I'm finna step into this store, Destiny said to excuse herself. She was still stuck on the fact that her friend she had known her whole life had never shown her criminal side. Destiny looked up and couldn't believe her eyes. The same thong bikini she had seen on the website was on the mannequin in front of her. She walked towards it, and on the shelves underneath where all the merchandise was, she saw exactly what she was looking for.

CHAPTER12

"Dad, please tell me you got something for me to eat." "We know you turn into a ravenous animal if you are not fed. Destiny quipped." "Shut up, Destiny. Pops, what you got?" I gotta keep my champ fueled. Here, big boy meal. "Thanks, pops. With a mouth full of fries, Future joked, "So, how many selfies and I would nerve you been through today pops?" It was cool. Destiny met with her friend Chanelle and her sister Keisha. "Omg, Dad, that girl is a stalker." Don't try and play Chanelle. Destiny warned. "And all my friends be thirsty for your long neck, and I have no idea why." "She was pretty to me, Ro stated." "I know you got the player gene in you." Say it with me, you ain't no player, Destiny said, copying one of her favorite movies. I am a player, a ball player. So, you finally got a swimsuit you like so I can stop hearing I'mma be fabulous and girl, what are you wearing? "Yeah, thanks to dad." Anything for my princess. Destiny was feeling so bad. She knew she was perfect in her dad's eyes.

CHAPTER13

"Future, you gone run to the store for me?" "I got you, dad. What do you want me to get?" "Get some two liters and a couple of bags of chips." Ro pulled out his wallet. "Here, a ten. Get you and your sister something." Future gladly took the bill. "D, Future shouted. I'm finna go to the store. You want something?" "Get me a fruit cup; she called back. Slim Jim." "Got it! Jokes, huh?" Destiny was not amused. "I'm out, dad." Ro lived in a whole different world. He knew from talking to his father that his grandpa had grown up in this neighborhood. His dad also grew up in this neighborhood but was destined for better. He couldn't grasp why it was more liquor stores than Walgreens. Now that he thought about it, there wasn't even a Walgreens in sight. Future crossed the street and walked by so many abandoned houses. He knew only one abandoned house on his mom's block, and it wasn't one of these types of vacant houses. He walked the last three blocks in awe. You notice so much more walking, more than you notice when you drive by. He got to the front of the corner store and saw all the graffiti. This was definitely a blood set. "Future? Future spun around, his heart beating fast." Varis? "Hoopster, what are you doing on my set?" Varis asked. My dad lives around here. We're with him for the weekend, Future explained." I thought you were in jail." For a fight? I was out that night. I'm just suspended." Aw, Future replied awkwardly. "Fefe, we want ice sickles! Varis scooped up a Lil girl with the fattest cheeks, wearing only one shoe. Fefe, you said we were going to the park! Future hadn't noticed the four little kids, all between four and seven until the first one had spoken. "Who is Fefe? Future was smirking." "My OG calls me VV. My Lil brother, Varis grabbed the little boy and nudged him; when he was young couldn't say VV, he would say Fefe, so it stuck with my little brothers and sisters." Go get a popsicle and find yo shoe. Varis said to his little sister. I left it so it can keep our spot in line, she explained. You crazy girl. All of them yo siblings? Yeah, but my pops in jail for life, so I'm all they got. Well, when my mom is home, it's me and her, but most of the time, it's just me. How many siblings have you got? It's just Destiny and me. Varis and

Future left the store with the little army in to

Man, I didn't know they just let you outta jail for a fight. Bro, we juveniles. It ain't guns, drugs, or robbery; we cool. That's why the set put me on so much, because I get at worse Bootcamp, then I'm out. They get caught, and it's a hard time in prison. But if you go away, Future wanted to know, who gone look after yo brothers and sisters? The gang, duh, Varis replied as if it was obvious. We are family too. Next man up when a soldier outta commission. Most of us don't have a dad, and some of us don't have parents at all, so the set is who raises us and teaches us to be men. Hey Varis, come here, boy. An older lady had called him. Thank you for finding my granny dog. You know she can't live without that mutt. You got a dub? Varis looked both ways, ran to a gangway, and jogged back to the lady and Future. Thanks, Varis. You get those kids inside; it's getting dark. Varis and Future walked away; Varis had a bulge in his front hoodie pocket. Future didn't want to know what it was. Bro, Future started; you're a kid yourself. It doesn't ever feel too much? Varis looked resigned. What choice have I got? I make sure my brothers and sisters go to school and daycare, plus I go to school. I know slime who can't even afford to go to school. It's life around here. Man, I had no idea. I always thought you were just a hoodlum. I get that a lot, Varis shrugged. They came across a dumpster with a crip gang symbol. Varis reached into his front pocket. Future flinched. Varis pulled out a spray paint can and painted the blood sign over the crip graffiti. Varis laughed. Man, bro, you jumped like this was a gun. Future laugh was shaky with nerves. You never know. Varis stepped back. Three, two, one annn swish as he shot the empty can into the dumpster. Kobe. Good shot. Why don't you hoop? I never had time for games. I'm gone, Future. Worm gone be out here tomorrow. If you can find time, you can come slime it a bit, Varis offered. My dad and I do this ride-around thing, but I'll catch you. Right. Woh woh. Future looked at the dumpster. His head was all over the place.

CHAPTER 14

"You got your sunscreen? Yes, dad. I got everything I needed. Gosh, you worse than mom." "I just want you to be safe and to enjoy yourself, Ro said paternally." Future hurry up, Destiny shouted. "I'm trynna be fashionably late, not miss the whole thing." Come on, guys, Ro ushered. After Ro dropped Destiny off at the party, he, and Future drove to the park for their weekly one-on-one basketball game. "Checkup, old man, Future said, bouncing the worn ball to his father. "Old?" You won your first game last week, and now I'm old. So how come you didn't want to go to the pool party? Ro knew he would have gone at Future's age." I don't like being around all of them people. It's like they are all fake. They always smile and be nice to me because they think I'mma be in the NBA, but they don't even know I don't wanna go to the NBA. I wanna do something else. It's like to be popular; you gotta fit this mold. I just know I'm different in my mind. Future felt like he was rambling. "I'mma never pressure you to do anything you don't wanna do. Whatever you choose to be, you'll always be my superstar. You understand?" "Yes, Pops. Now come get this work." And the game began.

CHAPTER15

One of the light blue lockers was buzzing with a cellphone on vibrate. "Hey, this is Jasmine. I can't make it to the phone right now. Please leave a message, and I will get back to you as soon as possible." Beep." Hey, Jaz, it's me, Trish Girl. I don't know what you got going on at home, but you gotta pay more attention to what your daughter wears out of the house. I'm not telling you how to raise your kids, but they're too young. Let them be grown later. Call me back. Beep. Her phone gave a short buzz and a text message alert. Text me or call me as soon as you get this; you are not answering your phone for anything. Beep. Hi, this is Jessis;-pe Russo's parents. I know we talked Thursday, but I'm not sure you understood what was on the invitation. Your daughter's attire was completely unexplainable. I understand you got a lot going on, and I can't tell you how to raise your kids, but I don't want my kids to be around that type of stuff at this age. Call me when you get this, bye. Jasmine's phone was blowing up with messages and voicemails about the party. But the E.R was packed. She was so busy that she couldn't get any time to check her phone, and by the end of her double shift, the phone was dead. By the time she got home, all she had the strength to do was pass out.

CHAPTER16

Destiny, there go your dad's car...
Quick. Quick before our moms realize,
Chanelle urged. "I can't believe you
actually had the guts to pull this off,
Paris said in awe. You're my hero.
You're the talk of the school year for
this one." "Come on, Chanelle urged
again before you get caught." Destiny
shuffled down the driveway and up the
block before her dad could all the way
pull up in front of the party. "Hey
princess, you have a good time?" Yeah,
dad, come on, I'm starving. Just before
he got all the way past Jessie's house,
Paris's mom caught Ro's attention.
"Hey, make sure you tell Jasmine to call
me." Destiny's heart was beating
intensely, thinking Paris's mom was
going to give her away, but Paris's
mom was so tipsy from long island iced
teas that it slipped her mind. "Alright,
bye. So, what do you want to eat, baby
girl?" "Nothing really," Destiny replied,
feeling safely away from danger. I
thought you said you were hungry.
Aw, yeah. Destiny had forgotten her
lie. We can get burgers. Ok. Burgers
for my babies. Future looked over at
his twin. "Pool party... You ain't even

wet." "Shut up, long neck." Destiny was so glad she didn't have to face her dad now. She knew it was going to come out, but she also knew it was going to hurt her dad's heart. She was his princess. That was worse than any punishment her mom was going to give her.

CHAPTER17

"Goodnight, Future." "Goodnight, princess." Ro stood at their doors, straddling the thin wall their rooms shared. "I know I won't be around all the time like before, but the best part of my weeks is when I get to spend time with the fruit of my loins." "Ugh, Dad, you always make it sound so vivid," Destiny groaned. "Shut up, D. I like when he uses that old-school game." "But for real, you guys are so big and beautiful. Ya'll, my most prized possessions. I came from this neighborhood. My dad came from this neighborhood. I ain't never had a lot, but since I had ya'll, I feel like the richest man in the world." "Dad, grandpa, was from these blocks right here?" Future asked, "Yeah, his whole life. Don't tell yo mom I told you this, but your granddad was one of the founders of the pyru-bloods. He was a community activist and served his country. But when he came home, he made sure I never had to go through what he went through. Your mom will be here in the morning, and you know she's gone be on time, Ro laughed. Future sat up all night thinking hard.

He couldn't believe his grandpa was a gang member. He wrote the sign he had seen Varis spray paint on the dumpster. He was really starting to like the color red.

CHAPTER 18

Ro had really loved Jasmine. She had been his only true love since they were kids. He thought she was stunningly beautiful. She glowed in the sun and had these big, beautiful eyes that caught your attention immediately. She was just a ball of fire who overreacted and could not be told anything different. He hated being on the other side of an argument from her. "What are you talking about, Jasmine?" "I can't believe you. I told you to do one thing, and you couldn't even do that. I don't know why I will think I can have you do anything responsible, and I know you." The anger in her voice was fueled by the multitude of voicemails and texts that had mortified her when her cell phone had charged. "Jasmine, can you please speak English? It's too early." "So, you don't know nothing, Jasmine laughed ruefully." I'm not even surprised. Why did I wake up today with my phone blowing up with people questioning my parenting? Because of what our daughter had on at this pool party? Did you even watch her at the mall, or did you leave her alone to chase some female? I took her to the mall and watched her, just like you said. She was never out my eyesight, Ro said, not backing down. You'd let her fool you in your face, Jasmine condescended. "I checked the swimsuit out myself, a pretty one piece with a little skirt, Ro replied, defending himself." I'll be there in a minute. We're gone get to the bottom of this.

CHAPTER19

"The breakfast good? Ro asked as he refilled Future's cup with more juice. Come on, dad, you know your waffle is my favorite, Future replied with a mouthful of waffle, butter, and syrup. "How about you, princess?" "Yeah, daddy." Destiny was spending more time texting than eating." Why are you all on your phone this morning? Pops, she's always on her phone, Future stated between bites." I hope both ya'll know how much I enjoy spending time with you guys, and you can come to me about anything. You guys got anything you wanna share with me? Ro watched his daughter texting." No, pops, I think I'm good, Future said casually. What about you, princess? You got anything you wanna talk about? Destiny could feel his eyes on her. She couldn't even get any sleep last night, feeling bad about tricking her daddy. She knew she was as pure as gold to him, but she knew he wouldn't understand and couldn't take his disappointment. "No, daddy. Can I be excused? What's this Modern family? Future laughingly mocked. Shut up, Future, Destiny snapped. It hurt Ro to know that his princess lied to him, but he also felt sorry because he knew Jasmine would be having none of it.

CHAPTER 20

Hey, mom, Future called as Jasmine walked through the front door. "Hey, baby, go and get your things but wait in yo room until I call you," Jasmine instructed. "What's going on, mom?" Don't ask questions, just do what I said, she replied a little more harshly than she meant to. She was trying to save her anger for her daughter. Destiny, she shouted, get in here! Destiny knew her mother well and knew it had hit the fan. Yes, ma'am, Destiny replied, preparing herself." I'mma ask one time. What happened at the pool party? And to be clear, I already talked to every parent there. I just wanna hear your side to see if I'm raising a liar. Destiny looked over to her daddy, expecting some help, but his face was hard, and he was paying attention to every detail. Destiny took a deep breath. All I wanted to do was stand out to Jessie. I didn't think it was going to be this serious. "Where did you get the bikini?" Jasmine's voice was sharp; Destiny mumbled; I stole it. Speak up. You know how to talk. Destiny was on the verge of crying. "I stole it from the mall." Ooh, so now you are a thief too?

Jasmine was furious. Where was your daddy when you were stealing? Cause he swears he was with you the whole time. In a small voice, when he left to help Chanelle's sister Kiesha. Jasmine shot a look at Ro so seriously that if looks could kill, he'd been cremated. He was staring in disbelief, stunned that his princess could commit a crime, hide it from him, get caught and hide that from him too. Stealing, Jasmine started ranting. "You could have been arrested if you were caught. Then you had the nerve to wear a grown woman lingerie set. I raised you better than that. What were you thinking?" Destiny was crying. I just wanted to look mature. Mature! Jasmine repeated that's not maturity. That's mannish; that's conniving. That's... That's hussy-fast girl stuff. Jasmine said, trying not to use the wrong words. I can't even imagine how those parents look at me now. What they think is going on in my home. You don't wanna know what I should do to you. But you are on punishment. No, forget that. You are going to jail. Lockdown hard time. I ain't feeding you nothing but bread and water. I'm turning your room into a cell since you are a criminal now. "Calm down, Jaz. I got this." Ro squatted right in front of Destiny. "You know why I call you princess? Because you are royalty, and being royalty comes with respect but also expectations. You disappointed me and came up short of my expectations. It's gone take some time to get me and your mom to get over this. That hurt, Destiny, worse than any whooping could have. Am I still your princess? Destiny asked through tears. "You will always be my princess, but you hurt me, but it's my fault, I trusted you, and you let me down." Destiny cried harder. She hated seeing that look on her daddy's face. "Save those tears, her mom cautioned." That might be the only thing you drink for a week. Jasmine sent Destiny to her room before she did something she would regret.

"Dang, D. Future exclaimed. I ain't think you had it in you, and you kept it away from me, yo twin." "Shut up, Future." No phone, school, then back to the room. Man, let me steal something; mom prolly three-piece me. Future started laughing, Destiny rolled over." Let me stop playing. But for real, D, you are a big dog. You got more guts than me. You know it's me and you against the world, but it's three people I'm scared of. Mom, dad, and Deonte were wilder and all for the same reason. They'll knock me out. I love you, D, goodnight. Destiny pulled the blanket over her face. All she could see was the look on her dad's face.

CHAPTER21

"What up, Worm?" What's Brackin, Future? "Stop talking like that, Worm; you sound stupid." I'm getting it down the pack; Worm said self-consciously. Is it me, or is everybody on their phones? Yeah, Future noticed, like they know something we don't know. "I hope it's not my aunties Facebook or I'm ruined," Worm joked. "Stop playing, Worm." Hey, what up, Brandon? What are you looking at? Brandon tried to pull his phone back, but Future was too quick. "Gone on, bro. Give me my phone back." Brandon was chuckling. "Ain't my fault; your sister got a number 10 with a large shake. "What you say?" Future's anger was instantly white-hot. Worm had to restrain him. "Calm down, Brandon backpedaled. I didn't take the picture. I was group chatted it. Future looked around. It seemed like everyone was snickering. He could only cringe, thinking about what Destiny must be going through.

CHAPTER 22

"Hi, Destiny. What's wrong with you today?" The school nurse was a pleasant older woman that every student adored like their own grandmother. I've been having horrible cramps. My stomach's been tight. Please, can I lay in here till school ends? The nurse hesitated. "I don't think I can do that. I can call your parents to see if they can come to get you. Let me check your temperature." A few minutes later, "you look fine to me. You think it's something you ate?" Probably, Destiny said, clinging to anything. Do you think it's, you know, the visitor? "No, ma'am. It's just my stomach. It might be coming; I don't know. I'm just in pain." "Ok, the nurse relented; let me call your mother and see if she can come to get you." She went off to her desk. Chanelle had walked into the nurse's office and sat by Destiny. You ok, D? "Yeah, she replied quietly," I'm ok. I just can't take any more of the stares; that's the worst. And the pictures make me feel so sick. I can't believe Jessie would even let someone group chat them pictures. Have you seen Jessie yet? Chanelle loved to gossip. "No, I would literally die." Well, if you ask me, you look fabulous, and two, I don't think Jessie like that, Chanelle said, hoping to cheer up her friend." I bet he doesn't even know who shared those pics. The nurse made her way back to the two girls. "Destiny, I talked to your mom. She says she knows what's wrong, and she'll be here in an hour to take you home." Ok, girl, Chanelle said. I got to get back to class. Everything is gone be ok. I promise. I heard they are changing your name to Saweetie. Bye, you're not helping; Destiny called after her. Destiny could only sit and think about what her mom was going to do, but she knew it was better than running into Jessie, she didn't think she could face him again until college.

CHAPTER 23

Besides the radio and the air coming from the vents, there was no noise in the minivan for the last twenty minutes. Jasmine glanced at her little girl, who was looking out their window the same way she used to when she was little. She knew Destiny was inside her own head. Her little girl was growing into a lady and was dealing with it by herself. She could only imagine how embarrassing school must have been today for her daughter. "I want to tell you a story," Jasmine began, breaking the silence. "Your daddy told it to me when we were young and had really started taking each other seriously." Jasmine turned the radio off. "There was this really old lady, very pretty, with long, silky grey hair down to her knees. She was a Lil plump and broad in shoulder. She had been on the plantation so long. The younger slaves called her queen because that's all she would say. Kings, queens. Kings, Queens. Queens don't lose their crowns. How, she would go on, her memory betraying her, how queens... how queens... She would say that so much and had survived so long as a slave, even the slave master and his family would refer to her as queen." One day, a new shipment of slaves arrived. The queen could still remember how, as a little girl, she was taught by her professors how to identify the geographical area of birth of an African by the littlest hints. Like, how startled by or how intimidated they were of Europeans. All of a sudden, she locked eyes with a young, bronze-skinned female. The girl had a head full of flawlessly waved hair. The queen slowly let a single tear wet her face. As time went on, the queen started taking a little walk along the field's border. Because of her age, it baffled the slave masters how she had survived so long and let her know she would die one day." One day, the young lady was the first person done filling her basket.

As she started the short walk back to the gathering hole, the queen crept upon her so silently and swiftly it startled the young slave. "Congratulations, your majesty. You're a young queen, but you gotta," shhh... They know how valuable queens are, so you must keep the fact irrelevant. The young slave was confused but was starting to get what this crazy old lady was trying to tell her. "Listen, elder; I've never seen my homeland. I was born on a plantation. I don't know anything about any queen, anything. I have no family; all I have is my pain to let me know I'm not sleeping and this is not a nightmare but life. The old lady looked bewildered. You don't see your crown. You have no awareness of your nobility. You're born with a crown, not given a crown. Because man cannot take what he has not given without retribution. Then a bright-eyed smile came across the old queen's face. I get it. Ooh, my fault. I understand, queen. I mean negro, the old lady winked then shuffled away as swiftly as she approached." Every time the young queen would see the old queen. The old woman would crack a smile and wink. She would sit up at night and ponder on the words of the old woman. She'd play out multiple scenarios of how she would be and what she would expect if she was a queen. She knew two things for truth. Nature couldn't have made whites superior and blacks inferior. Nature decided predator and prey. This couldn't be nature. The whites worked too hard to maintain power while nature is not maintained but occurs effortlessly. You have never seen a lion writing strategies and working out to catch a gazelle. Second, she could look up to the stars and know the world was bigger and she came from somewhere else even though she had never seen it or couldn't name it. The Queen's words slowly started to change how the young queen carried herself; she took more pride in her work. She kept her living area more clean and orderly. She even walked with her head held higher.

One day she noticed the queen
exchange a wink with another young
slave. The girl looked nothing like her.
It annoyed the young queen to think
the old lady had told that to other
slaves and tricked her. So, one
afternoon the young queen got done
working early, so she could be the first
one walking back. The slaves were not
allowed to talk at work. She approached
the old woman on her walk back. Why
would you lie to me? You told me I was
a queen, she asked. Lie? The old queen
asked in a whisper, clearly devasted by
the accusations. Breaking her stunned
silence, the queen responded, I know
only the oldest principle, upon which I
coast this realm of life. And of them,
truth is the oldest. I know of no lies I've
placed upon you. I know, the young
queen accused, that you told that other
slave she's a queen, too. I know your
wink. The old lady looked even more
hurt. Jealously is useless, just a reason
not to explore the truth. A makeup of
anger, ignorance, and cowardice mixed
on the face of men that washes away in
the lightest sprinkle of rain. The old
queen continued, does her crown
cancel your crown? Does her beauty
devalue the worth of your beauty? Does
your hard work make her sleep easy, or

does her hunger make you eat more?
Then tell me the relevance to your
crown. No lies have been spoken. This
is known; two things can be true at
once. We are the true creators of
democracy. Equality is the same as one
tree, many colors, many pasts, with one
goal. One body with no part less
important. From the curious Egyptian
to the governing Canaanites, to the
Cahokia Moors who, by nature, choose
to clothe you and me in ageless
charisma and strength. Questioning
another kingdom is the beginning of
the death of your own kingdom. So
rejoice! The old queen commanded be
proud that you and all your sisters are
queens but shh. They will persecute the
royals because knowing who you are is
the only key to regaining our rights and
freed

Jasmine giggled when she finished the story. I remember sitting, staring at your daddy like he was delusional, and asking what that had to do with me. He said, you are a queen and, in that, are entitled to the utmost respect, and no outside force or opinion can change that. The only requirement is verification of your own crown, and your crown is worn when you carry yourself like a queen. Me and your dad's disappointment only comes because of our expectations. You're a queen, aren't you? Yes, Destiny whispered back. Then no person, no situation, and no embarrassment can strip you of that. I know it's gone be a little tough, but what doesn't break you can't keep you broken. Jasmine shook her head. She had learned that from Ro too. How can he be so smart but act so stupid? She thought. Now let's go get a mani/peti. Consider this a jailbreak, but back to the cell, you go as soon as dinner is over, ok? Yes, ma'am. Hopefully, can I get my phone back then? Not that far, Jasmine laughed. Just like your daddy, give you an inch, you take a mile, a bag of chips, and a two liter.

CHAPTER24

Man, Future, I hope you shoot better next week. The game against Roosevelt gone be tough. We gone need you, Future. "My head somewhere else, Future admitted. You know I'mma be ready." Ight, bro. Future started to change his clothes so he could get ready to go home and put an end to this day. Future realized that his teammate Justin was saying, God, bless America because he blessed her. Dang, Future, Destiny got it going on. What did you say? Man, watch yo mouth. Future was almost nose-to-nose with Justin. "Man, calm down. You not build like that, and Varis ain't here to save you now. Future was going to walk away, but his pride got in the way. I don't need anybody behind me, he told himself. He took a deep breath and stood in Justin's face. You heard what I said (Watch your mouth!).

CHAPTER 25

"Ouch." Stop moving; you gotta put this on to make the swelling go down. Jasmine said, fussing over her son." I'm ok, ma. Stop, he protested. "Your dad gone flip more when he sees this eye. More than when he finds out you suspended and gone miss the next game." I told you, ma, I ain't have no choice, Future protested. I'm not who you gotta explain to, here, hold this on your eye. She said as she gave him the frozen bag of peas. "Where are your suspension papers so I can show your daddy? They are in my book bag. Future touched his blackened eye. He couldn't believe that he hadn't thought the situation through all the way. I'm looking, Fut- Jasmine stopped dead in her tracks. She picked up a notebook that had a whole bunch of writings and drawings on it. She knew the signs she saw but prayed that she was tripping. Jasmine rushed into the living room. Future, what is this? She was on the verge of hysteria. Future still had his head down, looking at the worn carpet. It's my first suspension, ma. Calm down. "No, boy, look at me when I'm talking to you. Future looked up and couldn't breathe. Where... where did you get that? Don't answer my question with a question. Jasmine snapped. Just some drawings, ma. That's private; he answered half-heartedly. Private? Jasmine said furiously. Boy, you don't pay anything in this house. Privacy for rent payers. Where did you learn this? I ain't even gotta ask that question. So this what you were fighting over? No, ma, calm down. If you tell me to calm down again, you gone need more than frozen peas. Jasmine threatens. I knew I shoulda made your daddy do his visits here, but it's ok; this is the last straw. Future stayed quiet because he could only think of telling her to calm down. He did not want to go down that road. Can I go to my room? He finally asked. That's the safest place for you now. Future got up so fast; he couldn't believe he had escaped without being smacked. He had thought too soon. Jasmine slapped him right upside his head.

CHAPTER 26

Destiny heard Future coming and hurried up, ran to, and jumped into her bed. Future slammed the door, and from the other side, they heard. SLAM SOMETHING ELSE, I'MMA SLAM YOU. Destiny snickered. Be smack down on Monday, jasmine yelled from the living room. Look like you should have been bobbing and weaving. Destiny joked, you know, daddy says, keep your hands up, hahaha. Future didn't even want to think about what his daddy was going to do to him when he found out. What craig daddy say uhhh oh yeah... You lose some, you win some, but you live to fight another day. Destiny laughed hard. Shut up; it's your fault. I wouldn't be going through this if you knew how to keep your clothes on. How I got something to do with it? Destiny was baffled. I don't wanna talk about it. I'm tired and going to sleep. Seriously, I don't think you're supposed to sleep with a head injury. Destiny said, suddenly motherly. I don't care. I'm tired. Destiny felt bad. She felt like her selfishness was drawing in the whole family and causing them stress, all because she wanted to impress a boy.

CHAPTER27

Destiny and Future both hopped up simultaneously. They both knew that noise. Mom and dad were arguing. Future ran to the door. He turned the knob carefully and pushed the door open slowly so it wouldn't make a sound. "Move, Destiny whispered." I'm tryna hear too. She squeezed under Future. Shhh. You gone get me caught again. Destiny rolled her eyes. Look at this; the twins could hear from their doorway. Jasmine threw the notebook with the gang drawings on the table. Once again, she was shouting, you being stuck on stupid, not listening to a word I told you. I told you to watch Destiny, your "princess," and you were so focused on her friend, momma. It was her sister, Ro interjected. Don't play with me, Ro. Now you see this; it's because you do not care enough to listen to more than two words I tell you. You blaming me for this? Ro had picked up the notebook and started shaking it towards Jasmine; how? He probably saw this on TV or learned it at school. "Listen to yourself, Jasmine chided." Why do you think I pay this ridiculously high rent? To get my kids away from that environment, but it seems like the problem is their daddy. Slow or something and can't wrap his mind around leaving that trash of a lifestyle

"Well, you loved the lifestyle when you were riding round with me getting attention; Ro shot back, and don't forget where you come from." I never forget; that's why I hate it. I hate that my father left my mother by herself. All the hard times I never wanted for my kids, but you don't care. You prolly taught him what these signs mean and told him about his granddaddy's old lifestyle. You better calm down, Ro cautioned, "first off, watch your mouth. I would never put my son on no set. And that's my father you are talking about." "That's why I can't talk to you; you listen to what you want." Get on with your point. I'm trynna be patient, but I got stuff to do. Stuff? Jasmine laughed harshly. You don't got anything, let alone something to do. Ok, Jasmine, time to fact-check you. First off, I think you are more mad about me being with another woman than the swimsuit. And as far as my son. I'm glad he knows both sides. It's called reality for a young black man. And you keep bringing up the neighborhood... Gone head, say what you want at heart. You want me to come to visit my kids, not be the daddy hoping that bring me back crawling to your house. You predictable. Jasmine cut him off. Well, predict this. You can talk to the judge about where you stay cause they gone tell you your visitation days. That's how you want it? Well, do it then. I'm tired of dealing with you. I rather deal with them people than you. Ro left, slamming the door. Jasmine knew he was a good man but didn't know a better way to get her point across.

CHAPTER 28

Future slowly shut the door. Future preferred to think to himself in his head rather than out loud. He left the closed door and jumped into his bed, the top bunk. Destiny could almost read his mind. Ma and dad always argue. Come on, you know they gone be alright... ain't they? Doubt suddenly filled her. Future's head was spinning, but it kept landing on two words. Them people. I ain't never heard momma use the visitation as a way to hurt dad, and I ain't never heard dad say, "them people." Future, you are overthinking as always. You know we gone be going with pops this weekend. Future sat up. You believe that? Honestly? Destiny couldn't hide the worry nor answer his question. She felt this was all her fault. If only she hadn't worn that stupid bikini. Destiny burst out crying. I'm sorry, Future. I broke our family. Future jumped down to comfort his sister. It's ok, Destiny we'll be ok. But Future couldn't escape those two words: them people.

CHAPTER 29

Jasmine moisturized her face and turned off her phone. She just wanted peace right now. She made her bed and cleaned her entire room. She couldn't remember when she last had time to make her bed. Her mother use to tell her that to hear God clearly, this what you had to do. Cook a personal meal with no pork and no alcohol, clean your personal space to the utmost, silence is mandatory, and ask for forgiveness. It's polite to come humble when you ask for divine assistance. Jasmine knelt down on her knees just like her mother taught her, as generations before had taught their daughters. She locked her hands, bowed her head, and didn't think a word. She stayed still to feel God and hear His divine presence in a still voice. Dear heavenly Father, I come to you humbly and graciously as I can. Asking first for forgiveness for my short comings, forgive me for my sins. Forgive me for not having faith in you. Thank you for my health. Thank you for bringing me out of my self-hate. Thank you for my beautiful kids. God, I know you know all, so I don't have to tell you my heart is weak. I'm lost and can't turn to anybody but you. I can only trust you with this. I need my kids saved, God. Show them the way. Show me the way. Send me your angels by fleets. I need You. In Jesus' name, amen. Jasmine got up and blew the candles out. She laid down on her just-made bed and hoped that the Lord had heard her.

CHAPTER 30

D.. D.. Destiny! Future hated that she slept so hard. What, what? Destiny said groggily. "I'm up; I'm up. I'm dressed. Future chuckled. Calm down; it's the weekend. Why you wake me up? She groaned. You know I hate that. I just came up with an idea... Let's run away. Go back to sleep, Future or are you sleep talking? For real, Destiny. Future ran over to his basketball trophies. He grabbed his 7th-grade regional trophy, flipped it upside down, pulled the platform off, and pulled out a knot of money. Look, D. It's two hundred dollars. Future, where did you get that from? Destiny asked, suspicious. Saving a part of my allowance and cutting grass. He said proudly. We can use this as a start. We can live with Varis. He got his own house. Well, not his own house, but he can do whatever he wants. I'll learn the game and protect you. We can figure the rest out after that, he reasoned. Destiny couldn't believe her ears. Varis, Future? Oooh, my goodness... You really been banging? No, but I really talked to Varis. He is more than gang banging and fighting. He provides for his whole family. I've seen it. Why would we run away, Future? We're twelve. We're not adults. Punishment ain't that bad, bro. We have only been on punishment for a week. It ain't the punishment. I feel like we are breaking mom and dad apart, and maybe us leaving will bring them together to bring us back, Future explained. It won't be forever. I don't know, Future. Destiny didn't like the idea. Look, we'll be gone for a little bit; give mom a break, and give dad time to realize that he and mom have to work it out so them people won't take us from him. Where did you get this idea? I don't know. It just came to me, Future admitted. Destiny did want to get away from school for a little while. She hated how everybody looked at her now. How long are we gone be gone? I promise no more than the summer. Ok, Future, Destiny conceded. Yes! Destiny yelled trynna convince herself this was a good idea; shhh. Shh, you gone get us caught before we even get away. Let's pack, get some sleep, and tomorrow night we outta here. Future stashed his cash back into the trophy and climbed back into bed. D, don't be scared. I'mma always protect you. I know Future. And I'mma always take care of you. Get some sleep. Love you. Love you more.

CHAPTER 31

1001,1002,1003. Bmmm. Phone vibrates~ OG got down from the pull up bar. Bmmm. The worst thing about being immortal is that you can be the most organized person in the universe, but eventually, you just get to the point where you have too much stuff. Bmmm. I just saw that phone... where in the universe I-bmmm. Ok, I know. OG went into his kitchen, through the garden, and past the orchard to his marvelous humongous refrigerator. He reached its top. I knew it! He looked at the screen and smiled. The alpha, the omega. What do I owe this most gracious greeting? Ummm, hmm, OG grabbed a cup and dumped some ice into his cup so cold it vibrated in the cup. He strolled down to a small spring with water so blue and clear that you could see straight to the bottom. He scooped himself a cupful of water. One of Moabs descendants, this should be interesting. A beautiful falcon swooped out of the sky and landed on a branch next to OG. He scratched behind his ear, and the bird flew off. A thousand years from now? Why such short notice? OG had to check the mortal-time converter. That's about 24 hours, he said to himself. This must be important. You request, and I comply. Tell Noah my Ursus spelaeus just had new cubs. Big cubs are aggressive. The momma bears a little protective but tell him that the honey remedy worked wonders. A pause. Ok, I know you are busy. I'mma let you go. See you at Jesus' next birthday party.

CHAPTER 32

OG went to his closet. He had clothes from the beginning of time. Mammoth cloaks, pterodactyl shoes. Egyptian silk robes with encrusted, flawless ruby belts. Three-piece suits, big bell bottoms, track suits, kangoos. It was like a mall all of the time. OG organized his wardrobe by the period. He looked at his closet map and found the 21st-century section. I ain't had to put on shoes, shirts, or pants in a while. Prolly have to get a hat, too. The shine of the white in his hair always catches people's attention. It didn't help that he hadn't cut his hair in ten thousand years. He stopped right in front of the outfit that had caught his attention ever since he had been given this task. The outfit was timeless and in his favorite colors, all black with white stripes. Aw yeah! This is definitely the fit. And most importantly, it went perfectly with his ride. OG went to his stable next, well, garage in this instance. Time evolved even the basic functions of life, so horses turned into horsepower. OG's garage was vast, but he knew he had to fit into the times. He hated this time's flimsy new model cars. "Man, I can't arrive at their house with this. They'd think I was jeff Bezos or something," he said as he walked away from the Rolls Royce. He walked up to the smooth Red Camero but remembered that they were children, and he had to be persuasive to even accomplish the goal. A two-door car wouldn't be a proper taxi in their time. I got to remember uber. Uber. That's what they're called now. He finally found the car he thought was a perfect mixture of the golden seventies and the present time. Not old enough to confuse, but not new and fragile. Now the color, he had to make the right decision. Presentation is everything, but never more than for this generation. OG pulled out his key ring and clicked the nob. Before him was this beautiful 72 impala, all-black original. Just as spectacular as it had been on the showroom floor back in 72 when he bought it. He had always had an expensive taste.

CHAPTER 33

Sunday morning was a daze, but for some reason, Future was so nervous that he couldn't even meet his mom's eyes when she brought them their food or checked on them. For some reason, he felt like his mom knew. He and Destiny were really obedient kids. They'd been grounded before for little mischievous things but never for all-out rebellious or disrespectful actions. Future, you ok? Destiny inquired. Future was pulled out of his thoughts. Yeah, D. Ok, cause you look like you are having a second thought. Come on, D, I'm fine. And we are doing this, and everything gone turn out fine. Destiny was having second thoughts herself. She rarely agreed with Future on what to play on the radio, let alone something this serious. But as she looked back into her memory, Future always had been a leader, in his own way, and she had this trust in him she couldn't explain.

CHAPTER 34

Unc, as OG called himself when interacting with mortals, looked in the mirror. He hated wearing hats, but he had to admit that this generation had the best hats, especially for dreads. All these centuries, and I'm still fly, He boasted to himself. Unc loved doing his job, a special job just for him. He brought truth. Through history and visions, when the situation was serious, he brought truth and delivered it straight to the heart. He used the personal power of one's ancestral history. Truth can be found anywhere, but the powerful profit solely from ignorance and the diversion of the truth. They learned the power of hiding the truth and distracting others from the truth. But the truth is tricky and as old as God Himself. Sometimes not knowing the truth is a gift, for if the simple at heart saw it in its rawest form, it would make reality unbearable. But for those chosen souls who bare God's most potent traits, truth is a necessary component, like a map when looking for a paradise. History is truth recorded accurately to show patterns of success, defeat, overcoming, and underachieving. But history is controlled, distributed, and sometimes misconstrued at the controller's will. History has a funny way of repeating itself. But truth is powerful. It is respected and can seep through the smallest cracks and creases. As Unc started to type the coordinates into his historical G.P.S., he knew that he was going to do his job and do it well.

CHAPTER 35

I knew you were gone do this; Future
complained. Shut up, Future. We don't
know how long we gone be gone. Just
because we are running away doesn't
mean I have to be a hobo. I shoulda got
you one of those sticks and bandanas.
We would've been left an hour ago,
Future only half-joked. Just go look and
see if mom is still awake. Destiny
snapped. She couldn't believe that she
was really going through with this.
Moreso, she couldn't believe how calm
and prepared Future was. He had all
his stuff packed and even wrote a short
note for their mom and dad. She had
always looked at Future as an
immature little runt, but her twin
brother had changed her whole
perception of him. She was still
flickering through channels. Any
minute now, and she'll be dead asleep,
Future reported. I'mma lay down and
listen until I hear the channels stop.
Future jumped into his top bunk.
Destiny grabbed her favorite picture
and stared lovingly at it. It was of her
sitting on her dad's shoulders at some
carnival. She was clutching a big, pink
dinosaur that she had wanted so bad

that day. Her dad had won it for her. She hadn't had it out in so long, but she knew that she had to pack the dinosaur to go along with the picture.

CHAPTER 36

She is asleep. Future told destiny. I just heard martin. You sure? Destiny asked. Yeah, I'm sure D, Future reassured her. Come on; we got to get out of the house and settle somewhere before it's too late and before mom finds out and comes looking for us. We are actually going through with it and running away, Destiny told herself. She grabbed her stuff and her dinosaur, looked back at her room, and knew that there was no looking back. Her life was going to be different from this point on. Future had a feeling in his stomach, too. He couldn't put his finger on it, but this felt like a life-changing experience. Future opened the window, threw his bag out, and looked back at his sister. You ready, D? Destiny handed Future her bags. He had one; she packed three in her backpack and two carry-ons. Hers joined his outside. Future helped Destiny out the window. Be quiet, so mom doesn't wake up, he whispered. Destiny felt the wind and looked into the sky. It looked like the clearest night sky she had ever seen. The moon was full and bright. Future, inside, set the letter on his night- stand before climbing out the window and closing it as gently as he could. He hoped that his mom and dad would take heed and understand that they all needed some time away from each other.

CHAPTER 37

Now what? Destiny asked. Future grabbed her bags. If you would let me pack our bags. We coulda look like we were going to our grandparent's house or something. But no, we look like we got put out or running away. We got to try to find a ride and prolly find a motel around dad's house. Then get a homeless person to get us a room. Future had it all planned out. Mostly. Right as they began walking, they saw a remarkably spotless older model car just sitting at the curb, running, with an older-looking gentleman. He was wearing an all-black tracksuit with white stripes. The driver called out. Hey, you guys. Know who stays there? I'mma urber, I mean uber driver, and this is the location I was sent to... The house he pointed at was a new house. Sir, Future stated; that house hasn't been bought yet. No one stays there. Well, call me bozo... I was pranked or something. Why waste a ride, you waiting for someone else? Future just felt like this was a blessing. No. I mean, no, we don't have a ride. We were just about to call an uber. It would be perfect if you could give us a ride. We're

not going too far, and we have cash.
Destiny whispered fiercely into Future's
ear. He could be a murderer or a
kidnapper. Why do you trust him?
Destiny, look at the car, look at his
phone. Trust me, a murderer or
kidnapper ain't wasting no fly ride like
that on trying to snatch two kids.
Future turned to the driver. We never
got your name. Aw, yeah, I'm Uncle
James, but people tend to just call me
Unc.

CHAPTER 38

Future always paid attention, and as they rode, he found stuff that seemed weird; at first, it was Unc himself. His clothes were brand-brand new. His skin seemed like it glowed in an unusual way. The whites of his eyes were whiter than the whitest snow, and his teeth were somehow whiter! But that he could understand with all those teeth whitening products out there and people being health freaks. Other things didn't seem to add up to this man being an uber driver. His phone was like none Future had ever seen, and future kept up with all the technology trends. But then again, he hadn't seen every phone in the world. The car was just too nice, and the oddest thing was the feeling in the car. He felt uncomfortably safe, like a tank couldn't make a scratch or that if they crashed, everyone would be unharmed. Future, what's your destination? Unc asked. Hold on, Unc. Future was startled. What did you just call me? I said Future, Unc said, matter factly. Destiny and future just looked at each other and didn't say a word. To have a destination is to have a purpose. Ummm. Uncle James, Future started.

Just call me Unc. How did you know my name is Future? That's the name your mom gave you, or actually, your dad gave you. To be 100% honest, your mom wanted to name you Justice. How do you know my mom? Destiny asked. Future covered Destiny's mouth to keep her calm and to prevent her from saying I told you so.

CHAPTER 39

Future finally realized that they were in a car with a complete stranger and could really have been kidnapped, especially since he knew their names and their mom. Don't worry, Destiny and Future. You guys are in very safe hands. The statement made them more nervous. I'm just here to make sure you're safe and comfortable so you can make it to your destination. Everyone must have a destination, or there truly lost. Unc explained. A destination breeds purpose, and with direction and a little bit of guidance, you will find greatness and truth. Destiny and Future were still silent, but it was weird they both felt so safe. Still, a little shocked, Unc observed. How bout we pull over at this burger shack and talk more about this destination of yours? Without waiting for an answer, Unc pulled over to the burger shack. It was an outside diner with benches and tables with umbrellas. The best part was that it was open 24/7. When they pulled into the drive-thru, Future thought about yelling or jumping out of the car, but he knew that if he caused enough commotion, Unc might drive off with destiny or try to catch them and hurt them. I know you want something other than plain noodles and white bread, Unc chuckled. Oh, and plain Kool-Aid, no sugar. You're lucky. Her punishment meal was grits and warm water. Your mom, that is. How did you know what we had for... Future covered Destiny's mouth again! Unc got out of the car. Destiny, Future whispered. Don't talk; let him. We don't know what he can do to us. If he knows all this, it means he took the time to watch us. This is serious.

CHAPTER 40

Destiny knew that Future was right, but for some strange reason, she felt safe, and she knew Future felt it too. So, what do we do then? Nothing, Future replied. Just wait for an opportunity to run, both together, and get the attention of some adult or the police. Unc had gone to the other window for a second and had come back to the car. Hey, you guys want your usual order or something different? Future just couldn't resist asking: usual order? What's that supposed to mean? You know, the same thing you usually get. My slang might be a little off since I'm older. You know, your lucky order. You got it the night before you won the junior regional championship. I believe you scored 25 points, 5 assists, and I believe... Wait, hold on. Unc pulled out his phone and scrolled a couple of times and 10 rebounds. You ordered a double jalapeno cheeseburger, chili fries, and a yellow and red slushie for your school colors. Future was speechless. Not only was the order right, but so were all that game's stats. Whoever this guy was, his intel was on point. Destiny, Unc continued; your order has been the same since you were eight. Chicken fingers, fries with honey mustard barbeque sauce, and a strawberry shake just like Aunt Linda. He even knew about Aunt Linda, future told himself, in shock. He was starting to get scared, but for some reason, as soon as fear rose, Future looked at Unc, and the feeling disappeared instantly. I'll be right back. Anything else? That's fine, Future answered. As soon as Unc was gone, the twins conferred. How did he know our orders? Destiny, I don't know. All this is strange. The only option is to do what he says, Future decided. Unc came back with their orders. You guys wanna eat in the car? But it a be a shame to waste a clear sky like this. On nights like this, the stars are extra bright to guide us through the vibrations of the ethers. Destiny looked at Future. Future gave the nod to say that they'd eat outside.

They both stepped out of the car. Unc
handed them their meals, and they all
walked to a table, sat down, and didn't
move an inch. Unc looked humongous
but was extremely well proportioned.
Future thought he looked like a cartoon
fighter. The bench wasn't made of
metal or stone; it should have budged
when he sat down but didn't budge an
inch. Unc opened his sandwich like he
had never seen a cheeseburger in his
life. It had been a while since he had
enjoyed food on this plane of existence.
He prayed the quickest prayer he could
and almost swallowed the burger in
two bites and drank the entire drink in
one long, loud sip. He didn't
understand how they made sugar and
water so delicious, and he tasted sugar
when it was first created. You guys are
lucky to be alive in this generation.
Yawl's food is the best, music ok, and
entertainment ain't that bad either.
Future didn't even realize that he had
started eating and was halfway done.
Destiny had only her shake left. Why
were they so comfortable in his
presence? Unc, who are you? Future
asked. Aww, now that's a great
question. But what am I would be a
better question for your understanding

to be expanded! But I'mma answer your question. I am James William Dickerson, but through time, I've grown fond of being called Uncle James. I have the privileged of having a special reason to exist. In dire situations, at the request of the purest of hearts and clearest of minds. I appear as a thought, clothed in the flesh, to uniquely educate the youngest forms of universal greatness. A soul, no matter how small or large its existence in this life could be the complete opposite in the next. A soul is perfect no matter its path. But certain souls are perfect on every plane of life. They just need a little reminder, and what better reminder than historical truth depicted purely?

CHAPTER 41

Future could not arrange the words Unc was saying to make any sense. So what does that have to do with you kidnapping us? He asked bluntly. Unc wiped his mouth with a napkin. Kidnap? Woah, now. I'm just a protector and teacher with no malice in my heart. I just came up with a proposition from above my pay grade. Who is that? Destiny asked. Another great question! He has many names for many people. As many languages, he has double that many names. He is in all and comes for all. He sustains and extinguishes at the same time. He builds and destroys all for the better of the world. Destiny had so many questions. What does he want from us? Everything Unc said was overwhelming. Better question, what do you two want for yourselves? What do you mean, what we want? Future asked, confused. You guy's running away, right? It was Unc's turn to ask the important questions. Why do you say we are running away? Future asked defensively. This late, two young kids, all these bags. It ain't that hard to put two and two together. So what's this

proposition? Future was just trying to
go along with Unc long enough to get a
chance to run. Clearly, this guy was
insane or just trying to keep them lost
until he got what he wanted from them.
But Future still couldn't understand
how Unc had known that they were
running away. They had told no one.

CHAPTER42

So, ok, "if we believe what you are saying and tell you what we want, how you gone help us?" Future asked, getting impatient. Delicious, Unc said to himself; I need to come to this area more often, still reminiscing on the amazing food. "I can't intervene with your free will, but I can show you something that will make you understand the sacrifices that make your present so comfortable and your future so bright." And I can show you a little of the future so you can see the weight of even the smallest decisions of the present." "How you gone do that?" Future felt butterflies in his stomach. Unc didn't answer but instead reached out to collect the rest of their trash and grazed Destiny's hand. She instantly felt a rush all the way to her soul. She grabbed Future. "What, D?" "Let's go with him, she almost begged." "Why do you say that, D?" Future was surprised and a little worried. "Because you feel the safeness like I do. What could it hurt anyway? If he wanted to hurt us, he could have been hurt us. Destiny reasoned." "Let's go; I wanna see." Unc was back from throwing away the garbage. "Come on, Future." "Let me show one of the wonders of the universe, the surfing of time!" Unc said, almost in awe himself. They all started towards the car and the adventure of seeing their heritage.

CHAPTER43

Ok, Unc clapped his hands together.
"So, for the next step to make this a real
adventure, we must know our
destination." Unc tapped his H.G.P.S
on the dashboard. Time express, Unc
popped across the screen. Unc entered
his pin, and a map of what appeared to
be stars lit up across the GPS screen.
Then a fill-out tab popped up. Unc
typed in a couple of boxes, then pulled
out his phone. "Don't get all weird, but I
need a picture of you two." "Of all the
things about tonight, a picture is the
least weird, Destiny replied." "No duck
lips! Future joked." Destiny gave him
an elbow to shut him up. Unc pulled up
the ancestry app explaining now this a
little more in-depth than the one you
know. It goes into detail about where
you descended from all the way down
to your first ancestors when it was just
one hundred humans. Unc took the
picture and was instantly intrigued and
excited about this particular adventure.
He loved the north shores of Africa.
Through all time, it remained the most
beautiful place on earth to him. After
all, it was his earthly birthplace.

CHAPTER 44

"Ok. So, what we got here is double the fun for the same amount of trust and understanding." Unc started entering the coordinates. "What did the app say about us?" Destiny was curious. "Well, in the English of this age, you guys' ancestors originated from Africa, so that's where we'll start. The time is 1626. The location is the most radiantly beautiful place I've ever seen. Heck, it's the first place I have ever seen. Fez, the capitol of Morocco." "Morocco? Destiny asked." "Are we Moroccan? "Hold on, Destiny, Future interrupted." "The first place you have seen?" "So, are you saying we related somewhere down the line somehow?" "Wasn't it just like one hundred people living in trees in Africa then?" Unc gave a bass-filled chuckle. "I'mma answer Destiny's question first. The short answer is no. The long answer is that through time, communication became more complicated. As language developed, civilizations fell as powerful nations' agendas and propaganda spread. We've fallen so far from truth. Truth has become more perspective than facts." The location at the time was Maghreb, and they were called Berbers. In my humanly birth period, it was called Moab. But to answer Future's question, every living thing is connected by a string of the most fine silk. "It will be my honor to call your family my family." Future had to ask. Unc, "how old are you exactly?" Unc gave Future a wink. "Let's just say older than time itself. Or since they started keeping track of it, anyway."

CHAPTER 45

"Every good adventure needs good
music, Unc proclaimed from
experience. Any suggestions?" "I ain't
heard a lot of tunes from this
generation, but I like what I've heard."
"Tunes?" Destiny couldn't help but roll
her eyes. "Unc, you are old." Destiny
had always been the car's DJ. Future
couldn't deny that Destiny knew good
music. Laugh now cry later filled the
car. Unc started the engine, and when
they all settled into their seat, their
heads began to bob with the music. For
some reason, this feeling of excitement
hit Future. He always had a hunger for
education, but this was different. He
grabbed Destiny's hand. Destiny looked
at her brother, and he knew that she
felt the same way. "Hey, what ya'll call
this music?" Unc half-shouted from the
front seat. "It's called rap, but we call it
turn-up music, Destiny explained."
"Hmmmm. Turn up; I like that. Well,
let's turn up, then. Seatbelts, Unc
reminded the twins. Traveling through
time still requires safety." As they
drove, the roads slowly started to blur.
Unc clicked another gear, and then it
was as if everything, but the music had

stopped. The car's front window was like the stars, but they were closer than imaginable. It was beautiful, beyond words. Unc still bobbed his head to the music. Sometimes we laugh, sometimes we cry, but at least we know now.

CHAPTER46

The window slowly started to clear into a beautiful sight. The sky was so blue that it looked like a different color. It was so weird seeing Unc navigating through trees to a small field with what looked like a barn of some sort. Behind the little plot that Destiny and Future could now see was a farm. Stood in a magnificent city. Its wall stopped at a huge body of water that contained docks and boats. Not little canoes but huge boats with sails as huge as big houses. Unc pulled into one of the barns. It was like they were pulling into a parking lot, the way Unc drove. The only thing off about it was the camels. As the car parked, it was as if the horses and camels could see them. Unc noticed that Future and Destiny were looking at animals. "One of the reasons animals don't talk is because they know too much." Unc went into his glove compartment and pulled out two watches. "Because you two still have earthly heartbeats, you need these." Future and Destiny put on the watches. "Your human body lives on a certain plane of life, Unc explained." "As you live your life on its natural plane, your lives, as all mortals on the human plane, vibrate more quickly. You get caught up surviving, enjoying life, learning, worrying, and then ultimately passing on to the next ether." "You miss even the most obvious of things. These watches slow your vibrations so you can maneuver through time unseen. Time never was recorded or relevant until man was created. Unc mused, so time doesn't stop as long as man exists. The smallest mistake now can change the world as you know it in your current reality." "So, no one can see us with these on? Destiny asked in awe. Like a ghost?" "In a sense, but not a ghost. On this plane, spirits such as charisma, trust, and even love and justice use these ethers to spread their attributes throughout the world. It's their job. We work and learn far after we depart our flesh."

CHAPTER47

"Ok, guys, let's get going. Unc announced, rubbing his hands together." "Hold on, Unc." "I thought we were going to Africa... That city is huge! I thought we were going to the jungle." On the contrary, Africa is a pillar of humanity's development, Africa from ancient Egypt, where a good friend of mine escaped, to this beautiful city. Africa has made major contributions to the development of agriculture and initiated grand civilizations across the world. Without my friend's courage to tell the pharaoh let my people go, would religion and the power of belief be so important to us now? It was Future's time to share. "My schoolbooks show two things: dirty jungles and Lil huts and a Lil about ancient Egypt, like King Tut." Unc nodded. "The controlling of education is an old power of control you'll see used throughout history. Trust me, the great scholars of all time from all over the world know the interactions of Africa and its neighbors are the cradles of all life." "They produced the greatest integrations of civilizations in history. Egyptians,

Mesopotamians, Assyrians, Babylonians, Persians, Nubians, ancient Greeks, and Romans." "It's the main reason the world is colorful and beautifully mixed as it is today." "Greek? Romans? Like that 300 movie? Future asked." "Yes, exactly! Africans and the Greeks lived amongst each other. Racism is an old evil but nothing like in your generation. Division is another tool used to control. They traded, lived, laughed, and even conquered each other. Just like where we at now conquered Spain in earlier times. But let's go see this history for ourselves." As they stepped out of the car, Unc hit his car alarm. The car chirped and started to transform into a camel. Future and Destiny couldn't tell the difference between the car and the real camels.

CHAPTER 48

"I almost forgot. You guys are gonna need these to understand the many languages ya'll gone hear." Unc handed Destiny and Future what looked like ordinary EarPods with a sideways eight just like their watches. As they walked, it seemed that they covered a lot of ground in a short amount of time, as if weight and distance were irrelevant in this plane of existence. They passed a shore of boats getting loaded with all types of crates of fruit, fabrics, rugs, and chests full of various treasures. There were endless stands selling fish and freshly butchered meat. It was like a big, loud outside mall. The biggest surprise was the mix of people. There were what Future could only think of as Europeans being told what to do by what he thought were their masters. There were men and women as black as oil with skin that seemed to sparkle in the sun royally dressed with dazzling, big jewels. This whole experience had been so odd so far; Future decided to open his mind to rethinking everything he thought he knew. "If you ask someone to paint a picture of a slave, they would paint a black person in shackles. That is simply untrue." Unc had rambled as he was enjoying the sights. At the gate, seven men with turbans on their heads and covered in thick robes left with their spears. They joined a caravan of people who had different types of hats. Unc told them that it was called a fez. They were heading towards a magnificent domed building. They are headed to visit their mosque, Unc pointed out. "I know what a mosque is. Future chimed in. It's like a church for Muslims, right?" "Exactly! In some cultures, there is no differences in religion and law." "So where are we going? Destiny inquired." "To see how it is preserving a legacy. Unc replied." Outside of the mosque were shackled men, but destiny couldn't understand how these Slight-skinned people were African.

They had olive skin, kind of like her and Futures, curly silky hair, and these beautiful eyes. She looked over at Future and couldn't help but notice the resemblance. "Unc, how do these people get along now? I thought white and black people were always segregated because of racism." Destiny couldn't understand what she was seeing. "This is one of the oldest conflicts. That cradle of civilization I was telling you about earlier, which is now called Europe, Africa, and Asia, split during an earthquake of unseen magnitude. This birthed separation, discrimination, and racism. People have always seemed to destroy what they don't understand or what they consider different. In America, you guys learn Euro-centric academics. The map you guys see of the world is based off the Mercator projection. Scientists from all over the world have debated his depiction of the world for decades. When the original land mass broke, light, and dark-skinned people separated and grew civilizations on six of the seven continents. The conflict continued on all levels, with history and science as its biggest battlegrounds. Racism is in all institutions, education, law, and everyday work. In every culture, people in power have always tried to wipe history away or change it to fit their views. At its roots, racism is hate, and hate is as old as time. But hate and evil never truly win. Love and understanding always shine through time. Don't let history teach you right from wrong; it can only show you clear examples of the differences between the two, Unc concluded." "So, we're finna go to church?" "No, Future, we're finna see a small example of integration and how nothing is done without a purpose."

CHAPTER 49

There were six men with maroon fezzes accompanied by a man with the clearest black eyes who had on a white fez. After all of them said a series of Muslim prayers, they also read the laws, and after that, the meeting started. The affair at hand today is building the financial stability of our new regime. The slave trade between the Frenchmen has recently been extremely profitable, but they're now requesting the bigger, built, more durable men. Preferably from the southwestern or eastern parts of Africa. But since the warring in Ghana, it's been more dangerous and defeats the purpose. One of the men in a maroon fez asked to speak. May I offer a solution to this dilemma? The man with the white fez never seemed to even move; he just watched and listened intently. "Unc, Destiny asked, who is the man with the white fez?" "That is the sultan of Morocco, Moulay Al-Rashid ibn Sharif , Unc answered." "That's like the king, Future said, remembering the movie Aladdin." "Exactly, Future! A very powerful and influential man." The Ambundu kingdom was an extremely intriguing people, strong and proud. Even the women. They are located in a convenient area and are currently at war and at risk of being invaded or usurped because of their current political state. They would welcome some of our resources and assistance, the man in the maroon fez said to the sultan. Plus, we can send someone with a common goal, the acquirement of the weaponry of the European nations. The sultan finally stood up, hushing the entire room. "I shall make this trip." Another man stood. "This is still a dangerous trip." The sultan looked at the man and said "trust me. Their leader and I have something in common, the dislike of the Portuguese." "And we both are starting our kingdoms with all the odds against us. The meeting ended as it began." Unc and the twins started heading back towards the car. "Unc, why does the world seem so much; I don't know, pure, I guess?" Destiny thought everything looked as if it was in high definition. Easy, the world itself was the wonder before pollution. Now the world comes second to human interests. Destiny was in awe. "Now I understand the save of the world people on the internet. Dad calls them hippies."

CHAPTER 50

As their camel was transforming back into a car, Destiny asked, Unc, "what's the next location?" Unc looked at his phone and entered the coordinates in the H.G.P.S. The Location: Ndongo, present day Angola. Language Kimbundu. The Mbundu. These are the warrior people, strong, proud people of tradition. As he started the car, Destiny, "what's next on the schedule of music?" "Unc, it's called a playlist." Do you hear me calling blasted through the speakers. The stars captured the windows much quicker than before. When the stars receded, the car was following a huge caravan. This scenery was closer to what they had expected of Africa, but it was still more beautiful than what TV could depict. The first thing Future noticed was the connection between nature and the people. The same water that the rhinos, elephants, and birds drank from, so did the people. It seemed natural, not degrading like in the feed the children commercials. As if on cue, Unc pulled up to the little body of water. The little birds landed right on the roof of the car. As they all climbed out, Unc pressed his alarm, and just like that, the car turned into a hippo. It slowly crawled into the water and sunk so that only the eyes and the little birds on the hippo could be seen.

CHAPTER 51

As they approached a beautiful village, Unc told the kids that they were in "Launda." Now, this part of Africa looked more like a jungle. The homes and huts looked nothing like the pictures of Africa in their school books. These people looked fully connected with nature, and even though they were more modern than Future had expected, they were still rooted in their tribal roots. The way that they were gathering in this field, Future knew they were doing something important. Boom... Boom... Boom, boom, boom.... Boom... Boom, boom, boom. A loud drumbeat filled the air. A young warrior wrapped in light armor made of fabric and twigs held a spear and wore paint markings on his face. He stepped into the middle of the crowded circle. Future could tell that there were two different sides as they both had different paintings and marks on them. A chant filled the air. An intense ceremony was about to happen.

CHAPTER 52

A group of painted warriors guided out
a rhino that also had tribal paintings on
it. Unc told the twins that the rhino
wasn't fully grown, but it was still huge.
One of the soldiers held a red powder in
his hand. He yelled "THE BEAST
WILL KNOW! BE READY, BE
SMART. BE FAST. BE UNBROKEN."
The small warrior crouched and was
focused. The crowd cheered loudly. The
warrior with the powder put it under
the rhino's nose. When the animal
breathed in the red powder, it went
berserk. The other warriors used their
spears to keep the beast in the center of
the circle with the little warrior. The
little warrior took off at full speed with
the rhino running after him at a trout.
As the rhino was about to overtake him,
he sidestepped and rolled twice, barely
avoiding the beast's horn. The rhino
grounded to a stop, turned to face the
young warrior, pawned his humongous
foot into the dirt, lowered his horn, and
charged. The warrior stayed put,
bouncing on the tip of his toes. A
second before he was about to be
impaled, he dove and instantly
regained his footing. This time, the

young warrior charged the beast before it could recover from its near hit. The warrior threw a rope with a heavy rock tied to its end, and it landed before the rhino's feet. The warrior then swiftly raised his spear and yelled a goading. "Yah, yah, yah at the rhino."

CHAPTER 53

As the rhino backed up to charge, the warrior circled the beast so that the rocking of the rope was behind the rhino and the other end rested in his hand. The warrior saw his chance. He lunged, causing the rhino to rise onto his hind legs. The warrior pulled the rope tight and pushed forward, causing the rhino to trip on the rope and fall. The little warrior rushed the beast, deftly avoiding the animals thrashing. The tripped-up back legs helped. The warrior pounced on the beast and, in no time at all, had it tied up. But the warrior wasn't done. He went to the head of the rhino, pulled out what looked like a jug of water, poured it out on the rhino's face, and rubbed between the rhino's eyes and head. The animal slowly calmed and lay still. The crowd erupted with cheers as the young warrior joined the group that bared the same markings as he did. The drums stopped, and one of the crowds parted. On the shoulder of six of the biggest men, Future or Destiny had ever seen was a woman. She was beautiful, and the crown on her head looked like it had always belonged there. The throne she was sitting on that was being carried was moved in front of the young warrior. Another man from the other crowd came and met the crowned woman. "Queen Nzinga Mbande, you honor us with your presence at this simple training exercise."

"It's my pleasure. I once was the one performing these rituals back when the world was simpler, she responded, fondly remembering." "Who is this young noble warrior? The queen inquired." "Proudly, this is my daughter, the young lioness of the Matamba tribe Keba." Future and Destiny gaped in surprise. "Daughter?" They said in unison, utterly shocked. "That's a girl?" Future asked nobody particular. "Yes, Future, Unc replied." "Listen some more. The queen was speaking." The Mbundu welcome you and your beautiful tribe to our lands and embrace the joining of our tribes. "We thank you, queen, and you're brave, valiant actions during the battle with the pale skin. You would have made your brother proud." "Thank you, the queen said with dignity." "Now, let us feast and dance till the stars guide our steps." The burly men picked up the Queen's seat and turned around to leave. "Unc, where's the King?" Future couldn't see him in the crowd. "She is the ruler, Future; Unc began his explanation. She inherited the throne when her brother was killed since his kids were too young for the crown. She was the most qualified and was quite extraordinary. A warrior, a scholar, and a stern ruler." "So, women were soldiers and kings this far back in time?" Destiny felt empowered. "Yes, Destiny. Women warriors have been making their marks throughout history." Future piped up, at school, we only learn about Susan b Anthony, Harriet Tubman, and Rosa Parks. That's American history. You have history past the shores of North America. Queen Sheeba, Nefatari, and Cleopatra, All women and all rulers, and all-important figures in history. "Queen, a man announced; we have a caravan approaching from the north." A rider has arrived ahead of them. "He says that they send their respects and that this unexpected visit is so important that the sultan himself has come." The queen's face showed little of her interest, but her eyes sparkled. The sultan of Morocco has traveled this distance to see me. This should be interesting.

CHAPTER 54

"What do I owe you for the honor to drink your water and to find food and shelter on your land, Queen?" "The honor is ours. It has been a while since we've had a guest from the North." "Queen, the sultan, **Moulay Al-Rashid ibn Sharif** has requested your audience for a sweeping hand from the queen cut the messenger's speech off. I need no explanation from one mouth of what another mouth wants to talk about." The man looked stunned. Destiny asked Unc why the queen had so aggressively stopped the messenger from speaking. "She has her principle as a ruler. Normally, the sultan would have come directly to speak with a King, Unc explained. It's customary. And she demands the same respect." The sultan floated as silent as an ant to the front of his guard and prostrated himself before the queen. "I apologize; he meant no harm. He is not aware of the customs of Ndonga." "I've read so much about your great people and have respect for your late brother. I, too, have read about your great Moroccan empire and pray for peace between you and your brothers. The queen replied, ushering him up from prostrating." The queen's wit was not to be underestimated; the sultan realized. Peace is a foundational part of life, but how seldom do we truly have it? "If possible, may we walk and discuss this peace? The sultan implied with a nod from the queen that she had three soldiers by her side. They had been stripped of their tongues; she reassures the sultan. They cannot read or write. Our conversations will stay safely between us." The sultan simply brought one Mufati, the most slender person in the area. "Unc, why'd he pick the smallest person to come with him?" "Danger does not come in sizes, Future, Unc advised."

CHAPTER 55

This land is so vibrant in color and pigment, the sultan mused. It's sad that distance deprives even the wealthiest of people of the experience of seeing all the wonders of the world. Enough small talk, the queen said, cutting short the sultan's musings. "You did not travel all this way for a view of the water you see daily." "Diva, ain't she?" "Shut up, Future!" Destiny watched, smiling ear to ear. "She very much admired the queen. I'm aware of your war with the Portuguese, and with the surrounding tribes who do not respect your claim to the throne, the sultan began." "I come offering a gift. A gift of power, gift weaponry to, let's say, even the battlefield." The queen stood silently. She stood like that until it became almost uncomfortable. Then the queen spoke. "A gift is given with nothing in return expected. Only a child or a fool believes in gifts." "Yes, but the exchanging of gifts is the whole economy of life and trade, the sultan countered." "And what gift are you going to expect in return?"

CHAPTER 56

"I would want the gift of flesh. How often do we send good, strong men to die, but how absurd is it that we never ask them to live life for us?" "I'm in need of flesh, but my people do not produce the type of flesh abundant in the Ndongo." "Sultan, the flesh is traded and sold all the time, but I can only guess as to why you traveled all this way in need of the build of my people." With a tinge of anger, the queen continued. "I will sell no soul to the pale skin nations for the fascination of my people." "If I may," the sultan resumed, trying to defuse her anger. "Only what needs to be said should be said. I am only trying to help both of us achieve the preservation of our kingdoms. All peace comes with a level of chaos." The queen looked to the sky. "Men and their religion, religion never solves conflict; it only complicates it." "Queen, I am only asking for flesh that would otherwise vanish in war. In return, you would get what it takes to reduce the amount of flesh that vanishes." The sultan turned to his sole guard. "I've become tired of my journey. I'll be heading back to the shores for a rest." "Queen, think about what peace is to you." He began to depart. Moabite. He turned back towards her. "How much flesh? I won't allow children." "The strongest only are needed, and women to replenish the strong," he replied. "Here in Ndongo, you don't receive what you cannot take." The sultan smiled, but in his head, he laughed. "Some take with their hands but the best take with their minds. I shall send word of my decision." The queen responded, then turned back towards her domain.

CHAPTER 57

"Stop running, you two." Kiba told her little brother and his friend. "Ok, Kiba," two little boys replied. She was still sore from earlier, but she remembered her lessons. She could hear her father's lessons in her head. Ease your pain by sympathizing with your enemy's pain. We never hurt to harm; we hurt to survive. We hurt to protect justice. The feast was extremely festive. This land had more food, and more wood for fires, and the smell of salt water was pleasant. Far better than the land they had once called home. The boy called out to Kiba." Come eat! I asked mom for yours, but she said that if I eat your food, the lions would eat me." "Get that out of your head, sister," he said, pulling her to where the fire was, her portion warm. "You made us proud, representing the Matambo way like that." Kiba loved her little brother. She was glad and a little jealous that he didn't have to grow up in war as she had. "I hope one day, he continued, you'll be like the Queen." "Kiba, you think you could control the whole tribe?" She patted his head before resting her hand on his nappy hair. He acted like he hated it, but she knew that was their thing. "Come on, then, let's go eat. I'll even let you eat the fruit I don't finish." For some reason, Kiba's mind kept remembering the worst part of times of war, the fire.

CHAPTER 58

The queen paced the shores, watching the stars. The night was pristine. How could a night so lovely bring a decision of ugly destruction? She thought to herself. The queen kept dwelling on the word peace. Since being young, she had always detested the look of hardship on people's faces. She recalled that same look etched on her brother's face. How she missed him. He was more of a thinker and politician than she would have admitted when he was alive. She wondered if she even knew what peace was and how to achieve it. She knew she had to find out what she had to do now. The queen wrote a simple word on a piece of parchment and sent it with her messenger to the beach where the sultan rested. Future and Destiny were quiet and looked shocked. The truth tends to have that effect, Unc thought. "You guys wanna see it all, the complete truth?" Future spoke for both of them. "I think we have to," he said hesitantly. "Are you sure?" Unc asked. "We could go to the car and skip this part." "It's ok. We got to see it Unc."

CHAPTER 59

One arrow hit the night sky, blazing
like a shooting star. Then began the
horns and then the drums. Kiba
sprinted from the hut, and there it was
a real-life nightmare. The night sky was
as if all the stars were falling to earth.
People were screaming, crying, and
yelling orders. But they saw no enemy.
Then there was galloping. Her father,
spear in hand, was foaming from the
mouth by her side. In a blink of an eye,
Kiba's world was changed forever. A
pale horse was galloping through the
tribe. She didn't know why its rider was
pointing an unsharpened stick at her
father. Then the stick exploded with a
boom; her father just fell. The whole
tribe was shocked into silence. More
horses, men, and exploding sticks
sweep through the smoke of burning
huts. That was enough to make Kiba
cry out-loud, but what followed took
her soul to another world. Kiba ran to
her father's hut, which had nearly
burned down. She threw the charred
sticks and barked away to find what
she feared the most. Tears streamed
down her ash-covered face. Her little
brother loved to sneak into her mom

and dad's hut so that he could hear the stories of the stars. How only the purest of the souls were allowed to become stars. She knew that he was now somewhere up there, shining as bright as only a star can. As she hugged his lifeless body, everything went black. The whole walked back to the car; Future held Destiny as she wept. It's never easy to see the truth, as necessary as it is.

CHAPTER 60

As Unc started his car, he looked through the rearview mirror and saw the depressed kids. He could skip the next part, but what justice would that be for the truth? The face of the truth wasn't always pretty, it wasn't served pleasant smelling or easy to digest, but it was the medicine that kept the body of civilization alive. For them to see the voyage it took to survive coming to America was essential to his journey of truth. But he knew that he had to lighten the mood, and he knew how to do it. "Ay, guys. This next location is slowly but surely, leading us back to your guys' future." "The future is the best thing you can have as young souls. It's a blank canvas waiting to be written by only you. That's the blessing of free will." The backseat was silent, in mourning. Unc picked the music this time. He thought he would go with the mood. Plus, it would make the next two stops easier to understand.

CHAPTER 61

It's been a long, long time coming, but I know a change gone come. Unc put on Sam Cooke's A change is gonna come. It set the perfect background for the rolling waves of the sea. The ship was like a house on water being guided by the wind and currents. The sight had Future and Destiny in awe. They never got to see a sight like this on the cruise their mom took them on. A pod of whales swam right alongside them. One of the whale's eyes was fixed on Future. "Unc, why is it like the whales can see us?" "Nothing under the sun is useless or idle, Unc taught. "Some physical matters, when needed, carry spiritual energy to their destinations." "Just like how a dog can sense a human's need for companionship. The dog carries love with him to cheer you up." "You wanna see the whale's job at this current time?" They nodded enthusiastically. Unc brought out his umbrella and handed the twins rain boots and hats embedded with a sideways eight on them. "We can't go out there," Destiny exclaimed. Finite minds can imagine. Infinite minds transform imagination into reality; it is

the key to achieving manifestation. Unc
rolled back the large sunroof, stuck the
hand with the umbrella out the new
opening, and told Destiny and Future
to hold hands and take his free one. As
the umbrella slowly began to float like a
balloon, the trio began to lift with it.
The twins felt like air itself and not like
they were hanging, suspended, over the
ocean. All of a sudden, the whales
emitted this low-pitched vocalization. A
mother whale swam directly under
them and jumped from the dark blue
water. As she rose, so did the umbrella
and the trio. Another whale leaped
higher. The mother jumped again,
twisting in the air before splashing
again. The group finally flew above the
ship. Destiny looked back over her
shoulder and saw the pod of whales
clearing out their blow holes. Destiny
took it as a gesture of farewell. Like Unc
said, she thought. "Every living,
breathing thing has a purpose, both
seen and unseen."

CHAPTER 62

The darkness was almost as unbearable as the rancid smell. Kiba had never been on a ship or had seen the pale-skinned people she had heard stories about. She would have been scared if the death of her family hadn't numbed her emotionally. The first day, the women were let out of the hull they were jammed into. They were packed so closely that when the person next to them relieved themselves, it would run down the side of their leg. It was worse if it was a person on a higher platform. Kiba found out quickly that they were not allowed to communicate with the men, especially in their native language. She had seen people jump overboard, get whipped, or even cut down for the entertainment of their captors. They had mixed all the captive Africans from all over the continent so that Kiba didn't recognize many and could only understand a handful. She stayed up one night listening to an old woman speak. She spoke of many ships headed for the same destination. The new world. A world where the plane-skinned ruled the world, and they were now slaves. They were fed the food of goats, and the fluid motion of the waves made many severely sick. Their captors had a simple solution for those too sick to cooperate; they threw them overboard to the sharks that routinely followed these ships. Kiba wondered what the water felt like. She wondered if her parents and little brother were waiting for her at the bottom of the ocean. When Kiba finally did get to sleep, she could only dream about the fire and the smoke. But the real nightmare was when she couldn't sleep and heard the terrors of the night. At night, the door would open. A bearded man with a lamp picks one, two, or even three women to drag up to the deck with him. When the women returned, they were so hurt that she could only hear their cries and screams. The older women would sing hymns to calm them. But the worst was the silence of waiting for them to return and them never coming back.

CHAPTER 63

Unc having to show and explain the journey to America was tremendously tough. Only one in every eight slaves brought from Africa made it alive to America alive. Unc stated. The ship slowed and became busy. Future noticed that a black man was on deck with the Europeans instead of in the hull with the others. Then he noticed the red fez. "What is he doing?" Unc replied that one of the biggest lost truths is that not all Africans come to America unwealthy, uneducated, and as slaves. Africans sold and traded their own people well before America was founded. Slavery is an ancient practice. Then they saw it. Land. The harbor was crowded with big ships with bigger sails, people loading and unloading ships, and flocks of seagulls. "It looks like a scene from roots," Future exclaimed. "Now that's another story within itself," Unc, laughed.

CHAPTER 64

Kiba could feel that the motion had settled down to almost a halt. Her heart was pounding in anticipation of what the new world would bring. Then she heard yelling. Women were being pulled from the hull, inspected, splashed with cold water, and then chained, shackled, and herded like sheep off the boat. This was the first-time men and women, adults, and children were all brought together. She knew she was just short of being an adult, but no one cared. She and all the women were fully exposed, grabbed, and groped like a Shepard examining his cattle's health. The life Kiba knew was over. She had been a princess and warrior who had faced a rhino, but now she was trembling and couldn't stop. In all this chaos, the flesh was being bought and sold. Kiba was no longer a person, just muscle. She heard very calm words from out of nowhere. They had been spoken in her tribal tongue. She heard, be strong, princess. This enemy is strong but not indestructible. Stay disciplined. Greatness awaits, but only if you are patient and strong. She looked around for the source of those words. She spotted a teenage boy, a year or two older than herself, with olive skin and the most dynamic eyes she had ever seen. The twins recognized him by his eyes. They had seen him shackled in the city of Morocco. Kiba saw that he was being bought by what appeared to be a husband and wife. The wife was gushing over the boy to the men, saying that she had never seen a slave with such perfect features. She had to have him, she begged. "How do you know my language?" "I've never seen you before." Kiba said. The boy told her, "I've been to many places and heard many tongues. My gift is my remembering bits and pieces of what I hear. I was born a slave. Your mind, your memory, becomes your greatest weapon." Kiba felt drawn to this boy, her only ally in a sea of people. If she was to be bought, she wanted to be bought with him. Although Kiba couldn't understand what she heard, the twins could. The white women, hot and hungry, asked for the price of the whole stock. I'm famished and can't stand this nauseating odor. The quantity is right, and they look like quality. "Please pay the man his asking price, dear." And with that, what remained of the boat's merchandise all headed into the new world together.

CHAPTER 65

Destiny felt like she had heard
something very similar to what the
colorful-eyed boy had said but couldn't
remember when or why. "Ok, guys,
now it's time to see another important
part of this war Unc announced."
"Which war, Unc?" Future asked. "Only
someone as special as you could ask
great questions like you do, Future, Unc
praised. The only war that will never
end but also cannot be lost. The
oppression of justice and love. The
battle for true freedom and equality. It
is an eternal battle; a hard battle fought
in the heart of men. We name it
different names at different times, but it
is the only real war between good and
evil. In this next part of the journey, it's
called civil rights." As Unc hit his
alarm, a pile of crates turned into the
car. The sunroof was still open.
Looking over Unc's shoulder. Future
saw the year set to 1963, and the listed
location was Atlanta, Georgia. In every
battle, there are always heroes. "Let's go
see one. Believe it or not, she affected
you guys' lives too." Now, Unc turned
to Destiny; "we need one of those feel-
good songs." Destiny giggled, and it

was futures turn to roll his eyes. Gunna's Sun Came out blasted through the speakers. The song set the tone as Unc took off driving through clouds. The sun casts a rainbow in the cloud mist. Forced to notice, Future couldn't believe nature's beauty. It was enough to convince him to start recycling.

CHAPTER 66

As the windows began to clear and they could see where they were, they were amazed by what they saw. The transition from one time period to another had been flawless and smooth. Unc pulled up in an alley. "Where are we, Unc?" Future asked anxiously. Future loved Malcolm X and Dr. Martin Luther King Jr. He loved learning about black history. He always aced his history papers even though he learned more about civil rights from his dad and from the internet than in school. But the chance to see that history in color and in real life excited him beyond words. Destiny was thinking more about who they would see because she had seen those slave boys' eyes every day. She woke up and looked in the mirror or at Future. The olive boy had been their ancestor; she knew it. She found it interesting drawing connections from her heritage. "This time, I'mma see if you guys recognize who we came to see," Unc challenged, pulling the twins from their thoughts. He parked in the alley and turned off the engine. When Unc hit the alarm this time, the impala became a trash can. "Man, Unc, that's the coolest car alarm system ever." Future said. "I just hope it doesn't smell like garbage when we get back in it," Destiny joked.

CHAPTER 67

It was like they were in a black and white movie, but it wasn't in black in white. They were in a small town, and it felt like the whole town was getting ready for the day. The twins noticed that the people who were opening their businesses were black and that they walked with purpose and importance. Destiny was surprised by how well dressed everyone was. She could see that they took pride in what they wore. She remembered her grandmother telling her how black people used to make it their business to never be caught looking dirty. Never give anyone a chance to see your struggle on you. Don't matter what their situation was like; they could be broken, but I ain't broken. Could be down, but you'd never know because I'd never show it. That's when destiny saw her. The hair was unmistakable. Her mother had always told them that they were given their full head of hair from their granny. "Unc, I think that's my grandma!" "Which granny?" Future asked. "Grandma Doris. I was just thinking about her." "Let me see;" Future replied as if his height could let him see above the street. Together, they walked across the street to the little shop. Future couldn't help but feel like he was in the movie **42** his dad had made him watch. "Hey, Mr. Marshall." "Hey, Doris." Future couldn't believe how pretty his grandma had been. She was beautiful in her old age, but now she looked like she could have been a model. "So, Doris, how has your dad been?" "Is he still working downtown?" "Yep, Doris replied, and still at the park too." Mr. Marshall shook his head in pleasant disbelief. "That man has been working hard as long as I've known him, twenty-plus years. And all his hard work gonna pay off when you've gone off to college." Everyone in town knew Doris was a straight-A student, and they were all rooting for her to represent them and succeed. She also ran track and excelled even with the schools integrated. "Now hurry up, Doris, and get to school. I know that ride across town is long and hard." Doris grabbed her lunch stuff and left Mr. Marshall with a cheery goodbye. Doris' commute was a mile walk, a short bus ride, and another half-mile walk to go to the only school that offered female track and field but also had up-to-date books. Her school was mostly white, and she had to work hard to stay at the top of her class. She had begged her parents to let her go to this school. She knew that her dreams of becoming a doctor and running in the Olympics required attending a good school. Doris always carried her nice school shoes in her bag and was never late for the bus or the school bell.

CHAPTER 68

The bell rang, and the class was let out. "Doris, can I see you for a moment?" "Yes, Mrs. Langley." "I read you're my next ten-year future planning paper." "Look, Doris, you're talented and very smart, but I gave you this assignment so that you could be realistic. This version of life you wish for may be too much for a negro let alone a negro woman in this country." Mrs. Langley liked Doris, but Doris tried too hard to compete with her white classmates, and she felt she needed to put Doris in her place. Doris straightened her books in her hands and thought hard before she responded. "Mrs. Langley, I know that my paper is based on everything going perfectly, but I work hard and go above and beyond to be respectful. When I planned my future, I incorporated the changing in this country. If a slave wrote a letter describing future freedom, they could only imply that the country was becoming greater than what their current living circumstances were. With civil rights becoming more and more relevant, you can only predict what a person of color could achieve in the future." "Doris, this civil rights thing is just a faze. Something to entertain America." "It will fade, Mrs. Langley assured herself. Certain heights in America aren't meant to be achieved by a negro. I mean, a female negro winning a gold medal and a Nobel prize for medicine." "Come on, don't you think that's a Lil too much?" "This country is changing;" Doris persisted. "A colored man can go on TV and express an opinion. Educated colored people are achieving more and more every day." "I have to consider non-fiction and fiction when grading your paper. I'll pass them back tomorrow. You have a future, Mrs.Langley promised, but be reasonable. Being rational is an important part of success." Doris walked out of the classroom, knowing she was going to get an F on that paper, but it was going to be the best F and the first that she had ever gotten.

CHAPTER 68

"Unc, how could her teacher talk to her like that?" Future wanted to know. "That's the thing about war, destroying the opposition. There are people who don't believe losing is possible. But change is one of the strongest forces created. It is inevitable, but that doesn't mean that it doesn't come without defiance and denial." Future couldn't believe a teacher would call a student a negro. "Unc, how come she called granny Doris a negro straight to her face?" "That's just how it was in this era." "This specific war let humanity commit a crime that has a long way to go before it can be amended. The stripping of the heritage, customs, language, and religion of so many different descendants of Africa." African descendants have been called many names. "In America, they've been called negros, coloreds, blacks, and African Americans, among others. But none of those names are what nature gave them; those were just labels." "But the label never gives substance to its contents. You can call salt chocolate, but that doesn't make the salt suddenly sweet. The name on the label doesn't matter only the quality of the contents matter. Those words only motivated us to become greater."

CHAPTER 69

"Is that our great-grandpa?" Future asked. "He has to be," Destiny replied. "You both have the same big ears." "It must be where your height comes from." "Shut up, D." Future said, trying not to touch his ears. Doris came home to her father asleep on the couch with the TV on more often than not. She pulled the blanket that had slipped down back over him and kissed his forehead. She loved her father. He would have worked ten jobs to give her the world. In order to live in this neighborhood, he needed ten jobs to pay the bills and save for her college. They shared the same dream to send her to get a real good education. Doris also worked three nights a week at a diner to help. She had to fight him tooth a nail, fearing her grades would slip. She won, and her grades remained high. Doris, come in here, her mother called quietly. "I kept your plate warm. Hurry up; that's the last dirty dish in the house." "You know I can't lie down till every dish in the house is clean." "So that's where mom gets that nonsense," Destiny mused, shaking her head. "Except she makes us clean the dishes."

"How was your day at school?" Doris' mother asked. "Come, sit down, and let me live through you a little bit." Doris loved her mother's cooking. Every night she cooked, even if they did go out or eat at somebody else's house. Her mother always said, good food gave you a reason to be together, gave you a reason to smile, a reason to share. Doris wasn't really hungry, but her mom's good food always made her hungry. As Doris ate, her mother could read her emotions and comforted her daughter with one of her great stories. "You know my granny's granny used to be the one who collected the food for slaves." "What the master called trash." "She used to work her black magic and a little seasoning from a fellow warrior who was a house slave. But she never let the secret out. She would boil stew, always keeping everything around her cooking area spotless."

Said it kept the spirit in the food pure. She secretly put those seasonings in the food, and everybody would wonder how the food was so good. She even fed her soups to the master kids when they were sick. They always asked what she put in their food, and she would simply reply. A little piece of love. That's it, a Lil piece of my love in every meal. Them meals kept slaves strong and made them feel warm and safe. The only good part of them were bad ol' days, hard days. Doris sipped her iced tea. "Mom, did you ever think civil rights would be on TV? Or did you think it was just entertainment?" "First, civil rights have always been a part of black people's story." Her mom explained. **Moses** was the first to say "let my people go, in **Egypt**. **Harriet Tubman, Nat Turner**, and many more helped our fight for freedom and equality. Television is a tool, but it doesn't make our fight any different. Civil rights is not a TV show; it's a much, much older fight. Why do you ask that, honey? Doris' mother took the cleared plate and went to wash it. This teacher said that my plan for my future hinges on civil rights and giving more opportunities to blacks. Listen, baby.

Our family, from the oldest stories I remember as a little girl, has believed in the future being greater. Men and women in every generation have sacrificed their lives and dream for the next generation. To get them just an inch closer to that goal of freedom, equality, and recognition in this nation. One with no chains, no Jim crow laws, no segregation, just freedom. Don't let no teacher tell you the sky's not yours. The stars don't have a preference of color or race. The sky, and the stars don't have any preference of color or race. The sky, the stars watch over us all. It's for all of us to dream and make their dreams come true. "Go get some sleep, baby." Her mom said, drying the plate. "I'm tired myself, got that eat sleep creeping up on me. Gotta get your daddy to that bed to keep me warm." "Ugh, mom." It was a good thing she had already eaten. "You gone feel that warm beds different than that cold bed, one day," her mom said with a wink.

CHAPTER 70

"We see where you get them kankles from, D." Future started laughing so hard that he was choking, looking at his grandma. "Don't let the funny hurt you, Unc warned." "What did you say?" Destiny thought that was one of the funnier things Unc said. Giggles are whispers from the funny spirit of happiness. "Don't let it hurt you," Unc explained. Destiny couldn't help but giggle. Doris was stretching. It was Friday, so she didn't have work or track practice. She had a lot on her mind, and she would just run to clear her mind. The air rushing through her hair just made her feel better. "Hey, Ms. Reed." Doris knew only one person that called her that. Doris turned around towards her next-door neighbor. Mrs. Dorothy Heights was walking down her porch. "Trynna run to Texas real quick? No, just a light jog," Doris responded. "Did you enjoy your trip?" "Yes! I wish I could have taken you to hear Mr. Lewis speak, Ms. Heights responded. "John Lewis was blessed to be able to speak in front of large crowds. I could never speak in front of all those people." Doris loved to hear Mrs. Heights talk about civil rights. She watched the specials on T.V. and a lot of articles and books, but Mrs. Heights was on the front line. "Maybe I could go with you next time, especially this summer before I go off to college?" Doris half pleaded. "Which college have you decided to attend?" "I'm thinking still, but I know I want to see another part of the country and still run track at a high level of competition. Remember, Mrs. Heights advised you, make your decision for yourself, and what you picture for your future. I don't wanna take up too much of your time, but I really need to talk to someone besides my mom and her negro spirituals." "Sure" Mrs. Heights said, sitting on her porch step and patting a spot for Doris. "I have time". Doris joined her

"What made you commit to civil rights? Doris really needed to know. What kept you going? You know, what made it real?" "Good questions run in your family," Unc pointed out, putting his hand on Future's shoulder. "You know, Doris, I've been hosed, I've been jailed, bit up by dogs, pepper sprayed, outcast by pretentious establishments. Trust me; I've spent long, sleepless nights wondering if this is worth it or if it's even real. Shoot, not to mention all the money I've spent and not making money at the same time. Then I remember those chattel receipts I've seen and remember my grandmother's slave stories. I see how your father and plenty of other black workers work for a quarter of what the white men work, doing the same job, make. I see the faces of youth, like yours and the kindergarteners, who don't know what being a slave was like. They just have dreams that I call paint and futures that I call blank canvases, and black and white are colors that don't matter to them. I see women who fight just to get half if any credit. That's what let me know that it's real, cause their faces are real. A better tomorrow is real; we just gotta keep pushing to show people it's real. How did you find time with your life and all? Doris' schedule was packed between school, track, and work. We make time when it calls for it, Mrs. Heights said simply. Doris loved talking with Dorothy Heights; she was really her hero. "I wanna go somewhere with a beach and a lot of white people." "Why is that?" It was Mrs. Heights time for questions. Doris stood up and put her hair into a ponytail. "I love to see how they look when I win. I like seeing the bewilderment in their eyes. Thanks for the talk." Doris hugged Mrs. Heights. "You are beautiful, and the world is yours to run," Mrs. Heights said in parting. Doris jogged off feeling better than before about her future. She had people like Mrs. Heights fighting for her.

CHAPTER 71

Doris, you home? Yeah, dad. It's been a while since I caught you home before I headed back out, he confessed. "Dad, you are exaggerating a little now." "How are you gonna tell me what a while is? If I don't see my baby girl for an hour, it might feel like a week to an old man like me." "Dad," Doris rolled her hazel eyes; "you are not old. Dad, let me show you something." She brought out her English paper and showed it to her dad. "I got an F today, but I wanted you to read it." Her first "F," as far as she could remember. Her father was not only a working man but also a thinking man. He taught himself to read when he had Doris. He remembered concentrating and working hard to learn. Now he loved reading and loved nothing more than to read his only daughter's homework. "You know what? This is my favorite F, and this F can go where the Fs go." "Where, dad?" She asked, smiling. "On the fridge, like when you were little!" Doris hugged her dad. She loved his spirit and how he viewed life.

CHAPTER 72

Doris was woken by a loud nose. She was instantly alert. The house was normally quiet because her father really needed his sleep for work. The neighborhood was always quiet this time of night because the block worked. Future could see the flames. "Why are we on the roof, Unc?" "We need to be down there. That crowd is marching straight for my granny's house!" "Restraint is a part of patience," Unc counseled. "You are too young to remember. Distance is our best friend. And here's a hint. You two wouldn't be here if everything wasn't for the best." The crowd's goal had been next door to Doris's house. Destiny was grateful. As Doris crept down the stairs, her father shushed her. The house was already pitch black, and mother, father, and daughter were staring out their window. Her dad was old enough to remember lynchings, and his eyes were focused. That's when Doris noticed the gun in his hands. She hadn't even known he owned one, but there he stood with a rifle. The small crowd of white men and to the twin's surprise, white women marched until they were in front of Mrs. Heights house. "The N-thinks she matters. She thinks she can change something. She got other N-organizing and striking, not working. Asking for stuff like benefits. You monkey's lucky you're not still in shackles. Come outside, negro!" Mrs. Heights' lights were out, and her car wasn't in front of the house. Doris's dad thought about going out there, but his wife squeezed him tight. "No, just let them go, Billy," she whispered into his ear. "Let them do their bad and go." Future didn't understand why they used fire to cause trouble. He could feel it in his spirit; he hated that fire but knew he couldn't do anything to put it out. The mob threw cocktails and a torch straight through her windows. "You are hereby evicted, N-! Take your uppity family somewhere else!" Other families started to come outside to watch the flames as the mob marched off joyously. What stuck in the twin's minds was that when fire fighters and the police showed up to put out the fire, they acted as if it was a nightly routine.

CHAPTER 73

Doris woke up, brushed her teeth, washed her face, and instantly went to check on Mrs. Heights. When she went outside, Mrs. Heights was sitting on what remained of her front porch, drinking her morning coffee like so many mornings before. Doris sat down next to her and was silent for a while. "Are you ok?" Doris finally asked. "Of course, sweetheart. I'm safe and insured. Nothing was damaged that can't be replaced." "But where will you live now?" Doris asked. "You know the worst part of it all, Doris, is that I wish the fight can end with a simple house being burned down or just a real war like the civil war. But this fight is not a physical fight. It's a fight of the mind and heart, and that can't be easily won. It's gonna take time and persistence." Mrs. Heights sighed. "I got to finish salvaging what I can so I can pack up." "So, you're moving away far?" Dorothy turned to face Doris. "I'm built for this war. I'm not running away. I'm moving right around the corner;" she said, smiling. Doris was so happy and wished she could rewrite her future planning paper because she knew what she had forgotten to put in there. She knew exactly where she wanted to go to school now.

CHAPTER 74

Honestly, Unc, TV does not do the style and fashion of the oldies justice, Destiny proclaimed. "Where are we going next?" "Unc, what would have happened if Mrs. Heights had been home?" Future asked. "Future, if people can organize a mob march with torches and cocktails, they should know when you are home." "Remember, Future, being violent does not mean you're strong, and fear is a more used weapon than violence," Unc explained. "You know how you kill a thousand foes without killing one person?" "How, Unc?" Future asked. "You kill their intentions. If you can remove the thought of even someone thinking they can challenge you, you remove the threat. Being upright, independent, and fearless, you can destroy the intentions of a thousand foes. That's why it was so essential for heroes like Mrs. Height, Dr. King, Malcolm X, Fredrick Douglas, and so many more to keep fighting through the fear. They helped defeat millions of enemies and saved even more lives by killing the intentions of the worst. Now, to answer Destiny, "let's go see where the next step of this journey leads."

CHAPTER 75

The car, thankfully, did not smell like the trash can it had been. Unc turned the G.P.S. on to find their next coordinates. The location popped up, and Unc knew that he was getting close to his goal. "The truth is simply the truth. Guys, we're getting close to home." "I got this. Unc, what music do you know?" Destiny asked doubtfully. "When you've existed as long as I have, you search long and hard for new music." As they rode off to their next destination. Never rains in California blazed through the speakers, leading them towards their ultimate goal. When the window cleared, all Future could think about was when he had snuck and seen boys in the hood at his dad's house. He knew it was set in California and on Crenshaw, but it looked like a different country. This looked more dangerous than Africa, and it was a good thing that they couldn't be seen. "Unc, you definitely gone need that alarm system in this neighborhood. To think of it, why do you even have the alarm?" "No one can see us." Just cause we're on another ether plane does not make us not exist". "We just don't live. Like I told you, we can't be seen, but even the smallest change in even how something feels can change everything. I know you guys learned about the butterfly effect. "Now come on guys let's go see the next part of this journey."

CHAPTER 76

"I guess me and my son ain't worth no fully cooked meal, just a plate of mush, huh? I fought six years to come home to nothing, to people who ain't good for nothing, for me not be worth nothing. I don't keep you happy; I don't keep this roof over your head." Ro was used to the yelling; he learned how to tune it out. His mom blamed it on his father's PTSD from the war and on what he had been through on the streets of Compton. Future was standing there with his jaw on the floor. Destiny couldn't believe her eyes. It was as if they were looking at another shorter Future minus the colorful eyes. Destiny couldn't believe her dad had ever been so small. Future no longer had to imagine what his grandfather had looked like in his prime. He remembered the visits to the old folk's home; that's what his dad called the veterans nursing home. His dad used to tell future stories of how Future's grandfather had fought for his country and sacrificed a lot for Ro to have a better opportunity. Ro always praised him for not abandoning his family, no matter how bad it got, and it got bad.

Unc, "how old is my dad?" Destiny asked. "Let me see... Looking at my clock, he'd be fourteen." "Calm down, honey. Ro's mother begged. I'll cook something else." "I need some air," the veteran replied. "I'll find myself something to eat." The twins never met their grandmother on their dad's side. Their dad was the youngest of three, both of his siblings' brothers. One had been killed while another had a life in jail. Their father wrote letters, visited, and sent money every two weeks. One time, their dad sat them down and told them about their uncle. Their dad showed them pictures and taught them that family was family until the end. That's all you got,

Till one day you make your own. You never turn your back on family. Future had even talked to their uncle a few times. His uncle was always interested in Future's basketball games. He bragged that he was where Future got his game from. Seeing their grandma made Destiny run her hand through her hair. She had her grandmother's hair for sure. Her granny looked so tired like something wasn't right. Destiny knew that her granny died before the twins were old enough to remember and that her father never talked about her. Ro would only say that she had demons that outweighed her beauty, and Destiny thought she was stunning. "I'm still gone make him something for when he gets back," their grandma said, half to Ro and half to the room. "I thought he'd like the hamburger helper..." she said sadly. "I'mma eat it, mom. Just make something small just for you two. I gotta go to work." He kissed her on the cheek; "I love you." "Uh-um, love you too." "Where's my purse?" Ro left the house on his way to his two-in-one job. He was too young for a real job, so he worked as a delivery boy at a pizza joint. He would also pay the cook to

give him extra pizza, fries, chicken, and
pop and would sell them on his
deliveries for way under the regular
price. He told the cook that the food
would be brought home to his family.
Ro liked his job. He got to ride his bike,
his prized possession, and the rushing
wind helped clear his mind. Plus, riding
the routes let him meet all types of
people. Sometimes they'd ask him his
age, and he told them that he had to
work and couldn't go to school because
his mom was sick. They would feel
sorry for him and tip him extra. It
wasn't like he was all the way lying. His
mom was sick, and this job did make
her better. He did go to school, though.
His jailed brother's words always
resonated in his head. School is where
the real money is. The girls, the main
events, the people who, years down the
line, gone make something out
themselves. Even if you fall flat, with a
smile like ours, they'll remember you.
Especially the ladies. Rio could preach,
but he couldn't use his own advice to
save his life.

CHAPTER 77

Ro came home at 10. It didn't matter much what time he came in. His dad would be passed out drunk, and his mom would be in another world. Today his dad was still gone, but Ro hadn't seen him around the block where he'd usually be when he wasn't home. His father was OG pyru and stood at his post. Sometimes Ro thought his dad did it just to be able to tell his stories to the young bangers so that he didn't have to dwell on his problems at home. Drinking, smoking, and talking about the good old days were his therapy. He was respected, and every pyru in the city, no matter their age, knew not to even speak to young Ro. Ro's father had already lost one son to the grave and another to the cage, and his baby boy was off limits. Ro's mom was dead asleep. He always caught her that way. Future was so shocked, he had grabbed Destiny's hand, and Destiny had a stream of tears running down her cheek. Unc hated to see people cry, but if the heavens didn't cry, the ground wouldn't produce what was needed for existence. Ro cleaned up the needle, put the cap back on it, and tucked it back into her purse. He gently covered her with a blanket. He didn't even know if she realized that it was him, not his father, who cleaned her up or if she really even cared. Ro took his night's pay and split it in half, stashing half in his mother's purse. She always made sure that they had food and that the house was taken care of. He knew how she spent the extra, but she was a different person when she didn't have it. She fought her demons best with the drugs. Without them, he didn't know what she might do to his father and to herself. She always thought he was too young to remember the marks on her wrists, but Ro had always been observant and didn't know what he'd do without his mom.

CHAPTER 78

Unc knew that what the kids had just seen was weighing on them, so he wanted to show them something else about being on this ether, how irrelevant gravity was. "Come on, guys, let's go see something cool." Unc pulled out his umbrella again and instructed them to hold hands. They all began to float higher and higher until they were above the whole city of L.A. At 10:30 at night, the city was a sight to see. "You know why having gravity is a must?" "Why, Unc?" Future asked. "Problems don't float. Anxiety doesn't fly. When you are up here, the problems stay there. But if everybody could come up here freely, how many of the world's problems would remain unsolved? So gravity and reality, mixed beautifully, keep the world grounded." "But secrets whispered from the abyss of darkness, talk to people through drugs, trick them into believing they can escape their problems by simply getting high," Destiny said. "The illusion of leaving all your anxieties and problems, even only temporarily, becomes a habit, and that habit makes people do things they wouldn't normally do. But battles are fought on many battlefields. Physical, spiritual, and mental. Battles are meant to be won, learned from, and to prevent future defeats." "Hey, Unc, look!" Future called out, pointing. Someone had been partying and was shooting fireworks. They were in the best seats to see the brilliant display of colors. Unc navigated the umbrella towards the colorful bursts of sparks. Being enveloped by the flares of color was a once-in-a-lifetime view.

CHAPTER 79

Ro came home expecting to get some sleep tonight. Maybe watch a little of the game. He was sure his dad wouldn't be home as he rarely was on the weekend. To Ro's surprise, when he opened the door, his father was sitting on the couch watching TV. His mother was lying across his lap as he stroked her hair, something his parents rarely did that Ro always loved to see. "Ay, baby," his father said gently to his wife, "get up for me, and go warm up some bath water. Let me talk to my son for a minute, man to man." She did so without a word and with love in her eyes. Ro threw his bag down and sat on the floor right by the couch, copying what his brother Rio used to do whenever his dad wanted to talk to his sons; it was either on the porch or in front of the TV. He knew he wasn't in any real trouble because otherwise, his father would make him stand attention like his dad did in the army. That would normally result in push-ups and burpees until Ro's arms were sore and as weak as wet noodles. "I want you to know how much I love you," he started. "I love you, and your mother, and I only get away, so I don't do anything I'll regret. You gotta know when to hold them and when to fold them, but you never get up from the table, you understand?" "Yeah, pops, I understand." Ro replied. "Do me a solid son, and never spread yourself thin. Never give up who you are in your heart for what other people believe is right; what they tell you is honorable. I gave my body for this country. I gave them my best years. I came back with demons and left the best parts of me over there. I never knew it would affect me the way it did. And you know what changed when I came back? What I fought for, or what I was told I was fighting for? His father pulled out a cigarette and lit it. Nothing, his father said bitterly. Nothing changed. I was still black, and I was still poor. What we did only counted for the people over there, and our brothers in the arm

The army's money was enough to get this house. Pay for my wedding, a car, and a good time here and there. I didn't know how much a family cost. I didn't know work would be so hard to keep. I spent years tryna find my place in this world and what I found next was just another war. But what was I without a reason to fight? I have been fighting my whole life. He took another drag from his cigarette. You know the first thing Mad dog asked me on my first day on the set? He asked me why they called it the army. Why do they call them marines, the navy? Why do they go to other places to fight the same problems going on here? I told him what I had learned to say in the army. He said, now you home, it makes sense? Was it worth it? Did it make you great like you believed it would? I really couldn't answer. He told me they sold you their dream with their license to kill. Keyword theirs. This pyru thing's ours. We named it; we control it. It's our people, our agenda. It's our status -quo. And you know what I did? I gave the last that I had for the set. I never thought it would turn out like this. We are destroying what's supposed to be ours, killing our people! Selling our people drugs. Turning our eyes from what's really going on. Tricked again after all that giving. What I got but you to show for everything I gave? Pain and tiredness filled his voice. Look at me! One son was dead, one son in prison, and not enough of me left to hold my house together. All I got is what I can see and the stories about what I lost. And you. They both sat in silence and stared at the TV as if the conversation had never taken place. Neither were actually watching the TV, both lost in thought as Ro's dad continued smoking his cigarette.

CHAPTER 80

Ro went to work early on the weekends. The weekends were always busy, and his side hustle always was better. He needed the money to pay for a couple of records he had his eye on, and his bike needed new tires. He was also saving for his first car. He was almost fifteen, and that's the age his dad got his first car. "Ay, Toni, hurry up with that order." "This Mccloud. You gone get my tip cut and maybe even punched in the eye. That lady can't wait for no food. I had seen her eat the box and all before." "Perfection like this takes time," Toni told the impatient Ro. "Ight, I hear you." Ro couldn't stop fidgeting. "You know, in some months you gonna be a real employee and the first thing you're learning is the meaning of hot and ready. Come and get this food and hurry back. It's jumping like double-Dutch in Lil Mexico." Ro was on his bike in a flash and was furiously pedaling. He knew Ms. Mccloud lived on the rough side of Compton. All sides were rough, but this was the heart of the hood. The jets were dangerous, but everyone knew Lil Ro, and he made deliveries here all the

time. Ms. Mccloud had the porch light
on. She knew her food was on the way;
otherwise, people in the jets wouldn't
waste power on a porch light. The
streetlights were enough.

CHAPTER 81

Ro was ecstatic that he had cleared out all of his merch and had even been given a five-dollar tip by Ms. Mccloud. When Ro had got on his bike, out of nowhere, a man with a black rag tied around his face jumped in front of him. The man pulled out a gun. "Break yourself, cuz," he told Ro coldly. Ro was so caught off guard that he let his bike drop. The masked man put the gun in Ro's face. "Come off the bike and run your pockets." He demanded. Ro was shaking so badly that it was a struggle to fish the money out of his pockets. Agitated at the time Ro was taking; the masked man asked, "what you tryna get me caught shorty? I'll lay you out," he threatened. "You don't believe me or something?" It happened so fast that there was nothing Unc could do. Future couldn't watch any longer. He didn't know what would happen. But he wasn't gonna stand by and watch his father get hurt. Destiny tried to grab her brother, but he was too fast. The gunman raised his gun and looked like he was ready to shoot when Future dove through the space between his dad and the gun. Ro put his hands up to protect himself. The gunman pulled the trigger, but the only sound that came out was a click. The gunman pulled the trigger again, but the gun clicked again. The gun had jammed. Ro pushed past the masked men and ran as fast as he could, never looking behind him. Future had his eyes closed, hugging the spot his father had been standing. Unc lowered himself and gave future a hug.

"To put yourself in harm's way to fight evil, no matter the risk. Despite all instructions, against all odds is the essence of every hero." Unc knew this young man was very special. "It's ok, Future. Come on, let's go." I think you have seen what was needed. Destiny wanted to make sure that her father was safe. When they returned to their grandparents' house, the house was dark. No one was in the living room. There were no police, no family meetings. They went to their dad's room, but he wasn't there. They found him sleeping in his parents' room, at the foot of the bed. His mother was flipping through the channels. The twins couldn't believe their father had the strength to hold himself together after all that, but little did they know, that was life for their father. Come on guys, one more stop, then home you guys go.

CHAPTER 82

"This is my favorite part." Unc proclaimed, smiling. "Now we go see what becomes of the future based on your present decision." Unc hit the G.P.S and started the car, which didn't need transforming this past stop due to the model's year. "You guys have power in your family; Unc went on. You have to remember every decision, every battle won by your ancestors. You guys are at a very critical point in developing healthy patterns for success. As these days go by, your choices will become more and more important. We're going to the future with your choice of running away having occurred." "Hey, Future, you ever knew why your parents named you that?" "Yeah," Future replied. "For two reasons. One, mom's favorite rapper was Future, but she said she was kidding when she said that. She said because she had twins and I would change the future, and D would help because it was our destiny." Destiny chimed in. "Mom used to tell me and Future that every night when we were real little, she said that's why it was important to eat our vegetables and brush our teeth. We had to be healthy for our big success. She used to tell us how hard she prayed for us to be great and how God told her we would be. We had to get a good night's sleep if we didn't want to make God wrong." "We'll let's see what the future holds, Unc said," laughing at his own joke. "You know any good songs by this future?" As they rode to the future, Drake and future's life's good blasted them to the final but most important step of their journey.

CHAPTER 83

Why are we at mom's job? Future loved his mom's job. She worked in the E.R and saw all types of injuries. You had to be strong and have composure to do what she did. He felt like nothing could faze his mother, except his father being late for something. Destiny hated the hospital. The smell was bad, but she especially hated the scrubs. As they entered the hospital, it was packed. They were waiting to see their mom somewhere. Listen, take the medicine the doctor gave you stay off of the ankle and ice it. You'll be back to normal in no time. Future couldn't stop laughing. Destiny was in shock. She couldn't believe her eyes. The future destiny had a ponytail just like her mom's and wore purple scrubs. What shocked Destiny was the baby bump, that was obvious. This was not how she had pictured her future. The future Destiny looked at her watch and walked over to the nurse's station. "Girl I'm finna go, she told the Asian nurse behind the desk. Call me if Kiesha still tryna sell her car. I'mma talk to you later, ok?" After their farewells, Destiny clocked out as her shift ended. She had to leave early

because she had a lot to do to get ready
and she was already running on about
four hours of sleep. When she got
behind the wheel, Destiny called her
dad. "Hey, dad, I'm so glad you up
early. You have that stuff for Future?"
Destiny asked her father. "Of course,"
Ro replied. "And dad I know I've been
getting on your nerves." "What's up?"
He asked. "I need gas money for the
week." Ro already had an extra
hundred already for his daughter. He
knew she was just barely making ends
meet with two mouths to feed and
another on the way, while still tryna do
school online. "I got you. What time
you gone be here?" "Give me about an
hour, gotta get out these clothes off, and
I'mma be right there." "Ok. Love you."
Ro told his only daughter. "Love you
more." Destiny said as she started the
car.

CHAPTER 84

Future destiny loved her children's grandmother. Ms. Barber was the best. She would let Future destiny drop off the kids early, and if she was late picking them back up, it was never a problem. Ms. Barber loved her grandbabies. "Hey, how was the kids?" Future destiny asked when she picked them up. "Just angels, Ms. Barber praised." "I don't know what I'd do without you," she confessed. "I love my grandbabies, and baby Future is one of the smartest children I've been around." It had been challenging taking in another child with her baby daddy already being in jail, but there was no way Destiny was gone let her nephew go to anyone else's home but her own. "It won't be much longer," Ms. Barber sympathized. "You gone have some help when Varis comes home." "He was a great father when he can stay home, Future destiny conceded." Future couldn't believe his ears. Destiny had kids with Varis. Destiny could never imagine herself with a guy like Varis. "I don't know how, but Future, you had something to do with this. I can't wait to see the future you. You prolly fat and a gym teacher," she teased. "If he stays outta trouble in there, he'll be home next month. His visit day is next week. You want me to come get you?" Future destiny asked her son's grandmother. "I'll see him when he get out. I can't stand them plastic chairs." "Ok, baby. Bye, my Lil angels," she waved to the kids. "Drive safe." Future always heard that it took a village to raise a child, she could only thank God that she had Ms. Barber in her village.

CHAPTER 85

"Hey daddy." "Hey, princess. How have these little monsters been?" "Hey, grandpa's big boys!" "Baby Future's growing so fast. Gone be long and lean like his daddy," Ro remarked. "How you doing, Destiny? You been sleeping and eating? I know you are eating for two." Ro rested his hand on Future destiny's stomach. "It's almost time to pop. I can't wait to see what you are, itty bitty." "Dad, I'm waiting for her father to get out. Stop playing." "I can tell by the shape of the bump that it'll be another strong boy, this time named after his handsome granddaddy." You promised already. "Daddy, you can't count a promise I made while intoxicated on pain meds at the hospital. Plus, I was delirious from pushing this head out," she said, rubbing her son's head. Ro pulled out the money he had for his daughter. "Thanks, dad." "You talk to your mom, Destiny?" "Dad, you know I haven't. I'm just not ready." You know, Ro started gently; "I never looked at your brother any different for any of his mistakes. I've never looked at you any different for any of your decisions.

Future, no matter what the circumstances, you will always be the heir to my throne, and you will always be my princess. I know you feel like your mother doesn't look at it like that; she's just hurt and needs time to process her hurt." "Time, dad? It's been almost two years. How much time?" Future destiny begged to know. "She just had a different vision for you guys' future. You know, and sometimes when people paint portraits, and it doesn't turn out how they visioned it, they don't see the beauty in it the way they used to." "Dad, I really got to get up here. You know the process," Destiny smiled. "I love you, dad, and I'll bring the kids by tomorrow to come see you." "You guys wanna eat some bbq from grandpa?" "Yeah," they replied, grinning cheerfully.

CHAPTER 86

Destiny hated going through what it took to visit someone in prison. It was bad enough that she had to have a background check. She spent over a hundred dollars a week on phone money for her brother and Varis. She even had to take in her nephew because Future's baby mother lost custody when she got arrested with Future. She would be released soon, but the process to regain custody was a long one. The worst part about attending a visit was getting searched. The drug dogs would do a walk-by, and the guards would look at her like a criminal. Future and Destiny had never seen a prison up close and personal before. Destiny couldn't imagine going to prison to see her brother. She joked a lot, but she could always tell that Future would be somebody. He took school seriously, took basketball seriously, and when he put his mind to it, he could do anything he wanted. Future couldn't wrap his mind around being a real criminal. He had so many questions that he knew Unc couldn't answer. He watched in horror as Future destiny went through the line to see his future self in prison. He looked at his future self. It didn't register what he could have possibly done to end up like this.

CHAPTER 87

Future destiny entered the visitor's
room and sat down. A few minutes
later, the visitation room began to fill
up with other people's families. One by
one, inmates started to join their
families. Future arrived, trying to be as
clean as he could be while locked up.
Even in a khaki one-piece jumpsuit,
Future stood tall with his head held
high like his father taught him when he
was young. Future destiny thought he
was so strong. Regardless of the
environment, he was calm and held his
composure. Future was a good man,
she thought. He just had a rough patch
after he lost his job. His baby's mother
had come up with a plan. Because she
was a manager, she thought it would be
easy to stage a little robbery, and no
one could get hurt. However, one of the
employees felt like Ebony had
something to do with the robbery, so
they reported her. The police ended up
questioning her and asked for her
phone records. She ended up coming
clean by being promised a lesser
sentence. She gave up Future. Between
the phone records and Ebony's
testimony, Future was arrested. For
two thousand dollars, Future and

Ebony lost there their freedom and their son. Destiny and her father mustered up the little money that they had for a lawyer. Uncle Rio kept telling them that a black man had no chance with a public defender. It took all her savings, but she wasn't going to lose her brother because of a flawed system. When her brother went to prison, she started reading along with him when he asked for a book to read. They had found a book called The New Jim crow, and it opened her mind to racial injustice in the judicial system. Future would tell her stories, and she couldn't believe what he was going through under the watch of those who were supposed to be the good guys. Destiny never missed a court date. She would even come early and stay later so that she could see the ruling on similar cases. The first thing she noticed was that her uncle was not lying-in public.

CHAPTER 88

Defenders' caseloads made it hard for them to focus solely on one case. This resulted in subpar pleas for their clients. It seemed like the nicer the suit, the better the deal. Future's lawyer was good, but since Future wasn't cooperating and he had brandished a gun while he tied up the employees, Future's best offer was four years. Ebony had received two years, with one of those suspended to probation. She was almost out, while Future still had years to go in prison. Due to it being a violent crime, he had to go to a high-security facility. The only good thing was that his uncle Rio was at the prison he had been sent to. "Hey, D." "Hey, brother. How are you holding up?" "I have been ok." Future looked tired. I was getting used to the deck I was on, but they needed my bunk, so they just up and switched my cell. On this deck, I really don't have anybody, so I had to lock up my box for a couple of days. Then the light in my room broke, so I refused to go in until they fixed it. But they threatened me with putting me in the hole since they ain't fixing my light any time soon. Other than that, I have just been working out, reading, and tryna keep my head clear and straight. How have you been?"

"It's been good," Destiny said, looking over to the play area. "Baby Future is getting taller every day. He misses you. He knows the times you call and will literally stand on my feet, all in my face, waiting to talk to his daddy." She laughed. "I told him you are my brother; he had the nerve to frown his face and say he's not your brother; he's my daddy. We almost fought!" "I had to explain to this young man that both were true. He only accepted it when I bust out the fruit snacks." They both were laughing. "Have you seen uncle, Rio?" Asked Destiny, "yea, I saw him two days ago. He is getting worse. You'd be surprised how many people love and respect Rio. I went and sat with him, and he was telling me how he used to think he'd never get to hug his brother's kids. He never got to have kids of his own, but his baby brother's kids were everything he could have wanted. Somebody to carry the family name to the next generation. He also told me something that made me look over some of my past decisions and hate the fact that I let myself get wrapped up. He said he could feel he was dying, and it was the worst feeling because he had so much, he never got to do. He'd been in prison since he was eighteen. Never got to raise a family. So much of life he didn't get to see. TV, books, and collect calls are all his life consisted of. Nothing to him was worse than seeing his nephew, the future of our bloodline, the one who was supposed to create generational wealth, in prison with him. He told me, it hurt my heart to have you see this part of evil, this place where dreams come to die. These guards had dreams, and I guarantee they didn't write on them what I wanted to be when I grew up on papers that they wanted to be prison guards.

They take what anger and spite they have from what's going on at home and take it out on us. The toughest guys you think of hate the mirror; hate everything they've become. They lie, they hurt, and they betray just because they can. If it's one thing you can do for me, nephew, it's to find a purpose. My worst fear used to be dying in prison, but now it's seeing you lose yourself and accepting the mindset prison can give you, that you're worth nothing to nobody. Future's voice was shaky. He had me up talking to the walls all night. It was messing me up, worrying over my purpose. I've got baby future, dad, and you, but you should see the guys that never get mail, or visits, or nobody to call. They're just lost like dead men walking. "You talk to mom yet?" "I told you before, Future, I just can't be around her or give her any conversation," Destiny replied, not expecting the topic to change. "I lost so much respect for her. How could you not be there at your only son's lowest point in life? No money on the phone, no help with your lawyer." Destiny was getting mad just talking about her mother. "She ain't never wrote you or came to see you. Trust me, I was upset with you about getting locked up, but I could never abandon you or disown you. We family. Then she went and married a dude. She really embraced his kids, and I just feel like he told her to shut you out. He's a cop and all, so I can just see him doing that. I told her that she should have come the day you got sentenced to see you, but she didn't. I called her after, and she tried to change the subject. I haven't talked to her since, and it ain't gone change until someone knocks some sense into her."

CHAPTER 89

Destiny went to get snacks from the vending machine and the boys from the play center. The kids were eating their snacks as Future held his son in his lap. He hated that his son had to see him like this but couldn't go without seeing his son for four years. He might as well get them accustomed to this while they were young. "You know, Future started, in here, I read and think, and think and read. I'm learning a lot about being selfish and how it's not just a word but how much it can taint your character. To build great characteristics is to eliminate selfishness. A part of selfishness is to not forgive, and forgiveness is a must in being great. Forgiveness comes from empathy, you know, to really feel sorry for someone. And I'm not saying forget. Whatever's on mom's heart that's got her feeling how she feels about me being here, I feel sorry for her. The conflict in her heart, the energy she has to use to trick her mind into that she's right. I know she misses her grandson and me, Future said with conviction. I know she takes pride in how she's raised us, and that pride got her willing to go this far with a grudge. You not talking to her only makes it that much worse. It's like she lost both of us. Destiny always listened to her brother. He was smart, but she could never understand why she had to be the bigger person. Unc wanted the twins to see how forsaking the principles you were taught as a kid could unravel one's whole life. "D, it looks like that baby gone come out any day;" Future smiled. "I'm tryna wait on Varis." "Yeah, I heard he's supposed to get out next month." "How did you know?" Destiny asked, surprised. "I just know, he winked prisons talk, words travel." "Visit times up," a burly female guard announced. "Alright, kids, say bye." "Bye, daddy," Lil Future said in a sad tone. "I love you, son-son."

CHAPTER 90

"Bye, uncle." "Love you too, nephew."
"D, I'mma call you tonight. Love you."
"Love you too, brother." Parting was
always the hardest part. They all
hugged, and Future walked back to be
searched. Future was rethinking
running away. Yeah, he was on
punishment, which he had deserved,
but he might have overreacted. He
could never let the fear of "these people"
turn his life into one behind bars.
Destiny had known that she had
wanted to go home after the first trip;
seeing this had sent her over the edge.
Unc was offering them a chance to redo
their mistake. All they wanted to do
was go home, hug their mom, and lie in
their beds. I wanna show you guys just
one more thing while we're here. Unc
said. Unc took the kids to the prison
yard. He took out his umbrella, and
they started floating slowly. Unc pulled
out his phone and tapped something on
the screen. Slightly above the prison
yard was another yard above that one;
this was another yard. But it was
women, children, old people, and other
young men. They were dressed like
they were free, but they were so sad.
Pain is a cord that binds so many

people to one source. You have prayers; you have victims, the family of the victims, and even your family. Unc explained. When someone is sent to prison, you imprison so many more by the hands of your actions. All their loved ones, all your family. Your dreams and hopes are all lost in this prison yard. Destiny and Future just looked at the yards, never wanting to contribute to this cycle of pain and sorrow. "Unc, take us home," Destiny said, for both of them.

CHAPTER 91

As they drove back in time, the windows slowly revealed the Los Angeles they called home. They drove by the burger shack where their trash still occupied the trash bins. They cruised through their neighborhood, and Unc parked in the exact spot he had picked them up. "Come on, guys. Let's catch the sunrise." "I wanna talk to you guys one more time." "Here, Unc," Destiny said as they returned the ear pods and the watches, thanking him. As the sun came up, the kids sat on the car hood, and Unc stood beside them. "You guys got to see battles; battles fought on different battlefields. It's been written that no weapon shall prosper against you. People tend to make those weapons physical and use those weapons momentarily." "There are weapons that are more evil than guns or knives. Evil doesn't live in a gun; it lives in the heart. But remember, no evil, no weapon will make you not be great. Leaning closer, I'mma whisper a secret from the other side of existence. The boss is not a man of mistakes, and we are his most precious thoughts made flesh. He would not waste his best material to be burnt in the fire. You are a part of him, and there is no part of him not meant for excellence. Unc continued, it is just a matter of finding where and when your greatness shall blossom. So a good fight is fought, but if everyone ran away, then surely we would know true defeat. But because heroes from our past and present have stood and fought oppression, famine, addiction, slavery, and even ignorance, you get to enjoy the taste of freedom. That's why we teach the stories of the battles. We teach the skills of what it takes to win the battles preserved by our ancestors. The battle is slowly but surely won. Place your eyes upon the wonders of the heavens and the sky; it will be a constant reminder of the endless wonders to be seen. It is also written that all that your eyes can see is yours to explore and enjoy.

Learn the truth; it will make you immortal and shameless. Learn love; it will make you legendary. Peace will make even your enemies bow, and it will extend your life. Enjoy being free. Freedom is to be enjoyed but respected. It was fought for and is a blessing to the righteous. Keep your foot in the house of justice. It is the home your mothers and fathers built throughout the ages. Remember, greatness is the path of all. Only you can let circumstances lead you astray. You guys have a glow only seen in a few families. Relish it, grow it, and let it shine. Future and Destiny saw how the sun began to give light to the night. They knew it was their job to keep fighting and not run away from their problems. With a grin, Unc asked, "you guys want the full length of my hair after thousands of years?" They both nodded, unwilling to speak and break the moment. Unc took off his hat, and dreads of pure light consumed the twins' vision. Unc was gone. Unc's job was done, and he never said goodbye. He knew it wouldn't be the last time he saw those two special kids.

CHAPTER 92

Future and Destiny both woke up in their beds with their bags still packed. They made eye contact. "D, I just had the craziest dream." The look she gave him told him that they had had the same dream. Future jumped down from his bunk, ran to his regional trophy, and dropped it when he saw what was under it. Destiny ran over to her brother. "What happened?" She asked. "Is the money gone?" Destiny asked anxiously "un-uh;" Future replied, speechless. Destiny picked up the trophy and saw a sticky note stuck to the bottom. "Thanks for the new music to listen to, Uncle James." "It wasn't a dream," Destiny gasped. They both stared at the trophy and the note. Then they realized that they heard their father's voice, but he wasn't yelling. Just wait till they wake up. Jasmine said. That's so sad. Everyone still out there, Ro said. Future and Destiny opened their door and joined their parents. "Did we wake you guys?" Jasmine asked. "No, we were already up," Future replied. "Just couldn't sleep good." "What's going on?" "You guys were talking, and we heard mom say something that was sad. What happened?" Ro didn't know how to break it to Future, but he knew he had to. "Your friend Rueben was killed last night, around the corner from my house. They are saying it was a gang shooting." Future couldn't believe Worm had gotten killed. Worm had been his only friend since first grade. Destiny knew Worm was a silly, harmless person. "Who would want to kill Worm? And weren't they too young for gang violence?" Future ran and hugged his daddy, starting to cry. Destiny hugged Future, and their mom joined in. Ro's cell phone rang, and when he answered it, the person on the other line was talking rapidly. "Alright, thank you." "Bye" was all the twins heard. "Who was that?" Destiny asked. "It was one of my neighbors. They said they found the person who shot Rueben, and the police are now in front of the house." Most of the parents are still in front of the abandoned house Rueben was found at, setting up a memorial.

Future thought of Unc. "Dad, I wanna see." Ro looked at his son in surprise. "Are you sure?" "Yeah, dad. I think we should all go," Destiny seconded. "Ok, you coming too, Jas?" "Yeah, I'll come. Hopefully, I can see Rueben's mom." The whole family rode over to vigil. There was a small crowd standing outside of the house, placing flowers and teddy bears in front of the house. There was even a picture of Worm. When they got out of the car, they saw Rueben's mother crying hysterically. His sister and aunt were holding candles. Jasmine could never imagine losing one of her children. Ro was thinking about something his dad had told him once. When you lose your kids to the streets, it's partially your fault because they didn't feel comfortable being at home. A parent's job is to raise their kids, not to force a kid to be what they want them to be. Don't matter the demons; their home should be their place to be safe. As the crowd had a moment of silence to remember Rueben, the police rode by three cars deep. Future looked up, and in the backseat of the middle car was Varis. Varis saw Future staring and put his head down. One of the police cars pulled up and parked. Two officers got out and talked to Worm's mother. When the officers drove off, Rueben's aunt had told the family. The family had been told that the young man in custody had been showing Worm how to use a gun that he thought was unloaded. Demonstrating, he had pointed the gun at Rueben and pulled the trigger. Rueben was shot in the chest, and the boy ran and left Rueben. The next-door neighbor heard the shot and called the police. Rueben's phone's tracking app led them to his bookbag that had been left at Varis' home. It was too much for Future, but he could only think of one thing Unc had told him. One decision is all it takes to change everything. We fight battles here and there, but we are destined to find ourselves where we can fight those battles best.

They rode home in silence for a while. "Ay, Ro was the first to talk, you guys wanna go get some pancakes?" "We can eat breakfast and sit and talk." Everyone agreed. As they all ate their syrup-covered stacks, Ro started to talk to his family. "I know it seems like your mom and I are hard on you guys, but it's only because we expect so much from you two. I don't care what the problem is or what trouble you are in; you come to us. We are family, and family is stronger than any bond you could build with a stranger cause we love you unconditionally." "And that goes for both of us," Jasmine added in. "Do you understand?" "We understand," the twins said in unison. "Now, you guys are still on punishment," Jasmine reminded them. "But how about today ya'll get a get out of jail free card." "And I barbeque," Ro added in. "It's been a while since I last cooked at the apartment." "I love you guys." "All of you," Ro said, looking right in Jasmine's eyes.

CHAPTER 93

Future! Future! Jasmine and Ro cheered from the stands. Destiny cheered with her friends in the student section. Future was on fire, leading his team with 30 points. Only 20 seconds remained, and Future's team was down by 1 point. The other team came down to court, trying to run out the clock. Future's teammate fouled the other team, their best shooter. The crowd groaned in defeat. The first shot was all net. The other team high-fived the shooter. He dribbled twice, focused, and shot the ball. The ball twirled in the rim three times and then somehow fell off the rim. Future's team rebounded and called a time-out. 8 seconds left to play. Everyone knew the play was for Future to get the shot. Teamwork on three, the coach yelled to the team. One, two, three teamwork! The team chanted in unison. They inbounded the ball. The point guard dribbled the ball up the court. Future rolled off a screen. 3, Future caught the ball, 2 Future stepped back and rose 1, and he shot the ball. It felt like the ball was in the air forever. All the sound left the building. Swish as the buzzer sounded. The crowd erupted! Future jumped up and down and was yelling "that's for Worm, that's for worm." Future wouldn't tell anyone but Destiny, but he knew why the other's team's best shooter had missed the last free throw. He thanked Unc silently because he knew he was there somewhere doing Future one last favor.

Afterthought:

If these words spark one conversation, stops one young soul from overreacting, and saves one missing child. It completed its mission and was worth every ounce of energy used to make this book. When I was a young child, I was adopted by my auntie and uncle. My mother has always been in my life, but for some reason, I never could grasp why we didn't live with her. I used to run away a lot. I always knew I was loved, but for some reason, I felt misunderstood. That is a problem that goes both ways and is the reason for so many missing young adults today. There has to be an open space to communicate and, as a young adult, be willing to have the courage to speak up. Don't feel uncomfortable about communicating. It's always worse in your mind than when you just express yourself. Adults, be willing to listen as a person with empathy and compassion but firmly with justice. Then understanding and accepting the truth, you build respect for your family. And remember you are loved even if your parents or kids don't know how to show it. According to The National Center for Missing and Exploited Children statistics regarding minors who have ran-away from home. Of more than 20,500 missing children reports, 90 percent of those are what are considered "endangered runaways." 47 percent of minors who run away from home report a conflict between themselves and their parent or guardian. Half of all runaway minors report that their parents told them to leave or knew they were running away and did not care. Females make up 75 percent of minors who run away from home and 80 percent of the girls report having been sexually or physically abused. 34 percent of runaway youth report being **sexually abused** before leaving home and 43 percent report that physical abuse occurred in the home. National Center for Missing and Exploited Children's 24-Hour Hotline: 1(800)843-5678. I was blessed with a real Uncle James in my life. Look closely, and you can find one disguised as a teacher, aunt, friends, parents, etc.

About the author:

Akeem Carpenter, a twenty-nine-year-old born in Chicago but proudly calls Hammond, IN, home. He is currently incarcerated in an Indiana correctional facility, working on becoming a better person and an example of it's never too late to realize your purpose to contribute to bettering the world we live in.

I'm Kia Carpenter. I am twenty-nine. I'm from Dolton, IL, but I reside in Calumet City, IL. I am currently a postal worker, and I have a beautiful son named Kai. My brother and I have so many more stories planned for the world to enjoy.

Pictured above: Akeem, Kia, and their aunt.

A HEART THAT BRIDGES THE GAPS

FOR ANYONE WHO WANTS TO
REACH OUT TO AKEEM WITH
WORDS OF ENCOURAGEMENT
ANYTHING U MAY FEEL LIKE U
NEED ADVICE, OR SOMEONE TO BE
A LISTENING EAR YOU CAN

REACH OUT TO ANY OF DIANE'S BRIDGES LLC SOCIAL MEDIAS OR PERSONAL LETTERS.

Diane's Bridge LLC

525 Main Street

P.O Box 120387

New Brighton, MN 55112

Best wishes and remember you are loved but it starts within!

Made in the USA
Columbia, SC
29 October 2022

70199089R00126